MON...

Welcome ...
Montana Ma...
and women discover love on the range.

THE REAL COWBOYS OF BRONCO HEIGHTS

The young people of Bronco are so busy
with their careers—and their ranches!—
that they have pushed all thoughts of love
to the back burner. Elderly Winona Cobbs
knows full well what it is like to live a life
that is only half-full. And she resolves
to help them see the error of their ways...

Thanks to his prankster brothers, Boone Dalton
has literally hit the jackpot. The strictly jeans
rancher has just won a new designer wardrobe
from Bronco Heights's most exclusive shop,
and he is fuming—until he meets gorgeous
makeover maven Sofia Sanchez. He thinks
she could be The One. But Sofia may call it
quits when she learns her simple down-home
wrangler is really a rich man in disguise...

Dear Reader,

This is my first-time effort in the Montana Mavericks continuity and what an honor to be able to participate in a world that has engaged many eager readers for decades. Bronco, Montana, is a special town and I was happy to get the chance to write about a certain cowboy, one of the "new money" Daltons of Bronco Heights.

Because of his brothers' practical joke, Boone Dalton wins a contest for a total fashion makeover and in the process meets the love of his life. He's the proverbial middle child, a peacemaker who smoothed tensions in earlier and tougher years for his family. He's still bitter toward his father, but when Boone falls in love, he'll find that he has a lot more in common with Neal Dalton than he imagined.

Not your classic alpha, Boone is a "horse whisperer" and there's a little bit of the cinnamon-roll hero in him. He's ready for a wife and children *when* he finds the right woman. And he believes from almost the moment they meet that he's found his future wife in gorgeous Sofia Sanchez.

But it won't be easy to get Sofia to settle down. Younger than Boone, she's got big plans for a bright future and career in high fashion. When she falls in love with Boone, she doesn't want to lose her grand-prize cowboy, but she's not ready for all he has to offer. True love doesn't just involve a rapid heart rate and sweaty palms, but a whole lot of compromise. And I had faith from the beginning that these two would work things out.

I hope you enjoy *Grand-Prize Cowboy* as much as I enjoyed writing it! Drop me a line at Heatherly@HeatherlyBell.com. I love to hear from you.

Happy reading!

Heatherly Bell

Grand-Prize Cowboy

—

HEATHERLY BELL

HARLEQUIN
SPECIAL
EDITION

Special thanks and acknowledgment are given to Heatherly Bell
for her contribution to the Montana Mavericks:
The Real Cowboys of Bronco Heights miniseries.

Recycling programs
for this product may
not exist in your area.

ISBN-13: 978-1-335-40810-5

Grand-Prize Cowboy

Copyright © 2021 by Harlequin Books S.A.

This edition published by arrangement with Harlequin Books S.A.

For questions and comments about the quality of this book,
please contact us at CustomerService@Harlequin.com.

Harlequin Enterprises ULC
22 Adelaide St. West, 40th Floor
Toronto, Ontario M5H 4E3, Canada
www.Harlequin.com

Printed in U.S.A.

Heatherly Bell tackled her first book in 2004, and now the characters that occupy her mind refuse to leave until she writes them a book. She loves all music but confines singing to the shower these days. Heatherly lives in Northern California with her family, including two beagles—one who can say hello and the other a princess who can feel a pea through several pillows.

Books by Heatherly Bell

Harlequin Special Edition

Charming, Texas

Winning Mr. Charming

Wildfire Ridge

More than One Night
Reluctant Hometown Hero
The Right Moment

Harlequin Superromance

Heroes of Fortune Valley

Breaking Emily's Rules
Airman to the Rescue
This Baby Business

Visit the Author Profile page
at Harlequin.com for more titles.

Barbara, my dear friend.

Chapter One

If Sofia Sanchez read one more contest entry from a frustrated wife, she would simply explode. This particular one, so much like the others, read:

> *Please, please, please choose* my *husband. He desperately needs a makeover. With better clothes, and maybe a haircut, he wouldn't look so disheveled. You have my promise that I'll* make *him wear the new clothes.*
> **Anna, (Tony's wife)*

"This is ridiculous." Disgusted, Sofia tossed the letter aside.

Sofia's boss, Alexis Huntington, owner of BH Couture, where Sofia worked as a stylist, had come up with the idea for the makeover contest as a way to promote their men's clothing and introduce a new designer line. But the cowboys of Bronco weren't exactly lining up for the chance to be dressed by fashion experts. Alexis wanted the perfect spokesman to bring in more men, and rather than hire a model, she wanted someone from Bronco. In exchange, the winner would get the wardrobe and agree to a photo shoot for publicity. Alexis had also mentioned possibly a billboard in town, showing the winner in a before and after photo.

"Another entry from a wife or significant other?" Alexis asked as she turned from the mannequin she was dressing.

Sofia would much rather be doing that, but in trying to call attention to her value, she'd taken on every dull task at the Bronco Heights boutique. She arrived early, stayed late and tried to make herself indispensable.

She held up another envelope. "Isn't any man in Bronco interested in a new wardrobe and a complete makeover?"

Sofia would have jumped at the chance to win a designer wardrobe. Then again, she only had to think of her brothers to realize that not every man in Bronco cared about the way he dressed. Most, no matter how wealthy, preferred leather, flannel, denim and cowboy boots. The men who did care about clothes, like the Abernathys and Taylors, could already afford them.

"Don't worry, we'll find the perfect man."

"Really? Will we?" Sofia smirked at the double entendre, because her boss was a bit of a flirt with their few male clients.

"You know what I mean." Alexis smiled back,

draping an emerald silk scarf across the mannequin's neck, then expertly tying it into a knot. "The man who deserves this wardrobe, who really *wants* it, will come along."

Sofia sighed. If they were to find this man, it would be entirely up to her. Glancing at the stack of contest entries, she briefly flashed on the old "find a needle in a haystack" saying. Somewhere in this big pile there was a man who deserved to win. Maybe the wardrobe would be all that stood between him and an executive-level position. She would love to find a man who needed this wardrobe, maybe someone from her side of Bronco Valley, where this could make all the difference to his future. But she wanted this *man* to write the entry essay, not his frustrated wife or significant other.

The whole point of the contest was for any man over the age of eighteen to win the wardrobe by writing or emailing to explain how a new look might help or change his life for the better. From there, Sofia would pick the most compelling and qualified entry.

When the doors to the boutique swung open, indicating they had a customer, Sofia glanced up from the next envelope. Alexis had decided to stay open later in October in anticipation of the coming holidays. Not to mention all the weddings of late. This month it was the big Daphne Taylor and Evan Cruise wedding, which Sofia would attend. She didn't have a plus-one, but she'd already chosen the perfect dress and accessories.

She walked over to greet a new customer who had just entered—an elderly woman. Sofia vaguely recognized the nonagenarian. This was the so-called "psychic" of Bronco Ghost Tours, the somewhat eccentric Winona Cobbs. She'd been recently reunited with her daughter, who'd been presumed dead, but actually given up for adoption without her knowledge. The sweet-faced woman whose arm she clung to must be her newly discovered daughter, Daisy McGowan.

With a glance in Alexis's direction, who waved Sofia to go ahead, she greeted them. "Welcome. I'm Sofia Sanchez, and I'm a stylist here. How can I help you?"

"Hello, dear. Aren't you lovely? I'm here to find the perfect dress. A very special dress for the Taylor-Cruise wedding," Winona said. "It's my great-grandson's wedding, after all."

"She already has so many clothes. I don't know *what* we're doing here," the other woman said with a wry smile. "I'm Daisy McGowan, by the way. And this is my mother, Winona Cobbs."

The older woman put a veined hand on her daughter's arm. "Hush now. I've told you that I don't have anything that *feels* right. I need a stylist." She turned to Sofia. "For me, it's all about instinct. Do you

have a sixth sense about clothes?" Winona cocked
her head.

Did she have a sixth sense? When it came to fashion, yes. And more so than anyone else in her somewhat conservative Latino family, Sofia did believe
in a muse. She believed in inspiration and creativity, and sometimes they came without any logical
explanation.

"Yes. Sure do."

Color, fabric, print, design lines and form. If that
was instinct, Sofia had it in spades. Her older sister
Camilla had an instinct and head for business, and
one of her three brothers was a born teacher. Everyone had their gifts. Sofia had been color-coordinating
outfits for the family since age twelve. For her mother
and Camilla, anyway. Her brothers wouldn't let her
near their flannel and denim. So they continued to
live happily fashion-challenged. Sofia loved them
anyway. She, on the other hand, adored the beauty of
a perfect outfit and matching accessories. And she'd
been accessorizing since grade school, so yeah, one
could say that she had a sixth sense.

"Then I trust you to find me the perfect dress."
Winona pointed at her. "There's something very honest about your face. I'm getting a feeling about you."

"My mother has her own psychic booth inside
Bronco Ghost Tours," Daisy said.

"I've heard."

Sofia led them to the back of the store with the

changing rooms and the mirror. A pristine white leather love seat and matching plush chair sat kitty-corner to racks of clothing and cases of shoes.

"Please, take a seat." Sofia ushered Daisy to the love seat, then took Winona's frail hand and stood her in front of the mirror. "Based on your lovely alabaster complexion, I'd lean toward white, black or blue because those neutral colors will make your beautiful white hair pop. But since this is a wedding…"

"No black or white," Winona said. "Blue sounds wonderful, but it has to *feel* right."

Sofia flipped through the racks, knowing the exact royal blue dress she had in mind.

"You're about a size six, yes?" She held up the dress to Winona so she could view it in the three-way mirror, and they both admired the way it draped across her thin frame.

"Right on the money with my dress size," Winona said. "That must take a special talent. But this just isn't right, dear. Darling though it is."

Sofia might not always get it right the first time, but she was always close. She could feel it in the air like the snap, crackle and pop of a thrill. She was in her wheelhouse. Flipping through the dresses, she turned to Winona.

"How do you feel about a bright pop of color?"

"I'd say you're speaking my language," Winona said.

Sofia had a sense that this small woman was a force to be reckoned with. She chose the long-sleeved red dress from the next rack, a simple and classic dress with a waist-defining tie-belt.

Draping it over Winona's form, she met her eyes in the mirror and smiled. "Deep inside, you're quite fierce, aren't you?"

"Not all that deep inside, but yes." The smile was returned. "*This* is the one."

"It looks like you and my mother will get along just fine," Daisy added from her chair. "You both have good intuition about people."

"You look vibrant," Sofia told her new client, "and I bet you feel powerful."

"I am powerful." Winona tilted her chin.

And, of course, she was. Winona was now part of the Abernathy family, after all, one of the biggest ranching dynasties in Bronco Heights. That kind of wealth and influence defined a person.

Last year, with help from her grandson Evan, Melanie Driscoll and a long-lost journal, Dorothea—known as Daisy to her family—had discovered that she was in fact the long-lost secret child of Winona and Josiah Abernathy, Winona's first love. Unfortunately, he'd died last year shortly after being reunited with Winona and Daisy. Though she'd only known both of her real parents for a brief time, Daisy was grateful to be able to share time with her mother, and the two were usually found about town together.

"Please try it on for size while I search for the perfect accessories."

Sofia chose silver flats and a black scarf to accessorize and had Winona try on the entire ensemble.

"I'm ready for my close-up, Mr. DeMille," she joked.

A few minutes later, Sofia carefully wrapped the dress, shoes and scarf, and Winona paid for her purchases.

While her daughter picked up the shopping bag, Winona zeroed in on the stack of envelopes near the register. She appeared to be in a kind of trance.

"Those are entries for the contest we're having." Sofia briefly touched the stack.

"That's the right one, believe me." Winona pointed to a blue envelope, just one in the stack of contest entries. "I can tell you've been searching. Well, this is the one you've been looking for. You won't be sorry."

"Why? Do you know who wrote it?"

"No clue! But it's the right one."

That sounded ridiculous. Winona couldn't possibly know the winning entry without reading it first.

"But…why this one?" Sofia asked, picking up the envelope, but Daisy and Winona were already making their way out of the boutique, waving to someone outside.

Confused but intrigued, Sofia opened it and read.

My name is Boone Dalton. I'm 31 years old, and I'd like a chance to win the wardrobe. I think I need a total makeover to finally be ac-

cepted into Bronco. My family and I moved here two years ago, but we're not well respected. Sometimes I think that maybe because of the way I dress, I get passed over. I know I shouldn't care what others think of me, but I'd like the chance to make my family proud. Looks can only go so far, but maybe I can finally prove to everyone that I'm someone they should respect.

Sofia's heart gave a powerful tug. How well she remembered years ago when a mean girl had made fun of Sofia's hand-me-downs. She'd thought the clothes she wore were beautiful until someone pointed out that they were "second rate."

"Finally," she whispered. "Alexis! I think we have a live one."

"Great." Alexis came to join Sofia, who handed her the entry. She read it, too. "Oh, my. Poor guy."

"I know. Winona Cobbs said he's the one! How about that? She just *knew* and pointed right to the envelope."

"You mean Winona Cobbs, Evan Cruise's great-grandmother? The lady who has a psychic booth at Bronco Ghost Tours?" Alexis shook her head. "I wouldn't go by her. Read all of them and see if you find another guy. It's only fair to read them all."

Sofia sighed. It wasn't just Winona's input, but she wanted to stop at Boone Dalton. Like Daniel Boone.

What a cool name. And the words just jumped off the page, his emotion and desire to be accepted palpable. There was a certain sparkle in that letter that she almost felt in a physical sense. But she shook it off.

She'd certainly never claimed to be psychic. It didn't make any sense to be drawn to the letter, or why without explanation she knew he *was* the one. She wanted to meet this man and help him earn the respect he deserved from whatever hoity-toity people in the Bronco Heights section of town didn't think him good enough.

She read the rest of the entries, all from frustrated girlfriends and wives, and one ten-year-old boy who wanted to impress a girl. Pretty cute but BH Couture didn't have a children's line. Something to think about. Sofia kept coming back to Boone. Time to make an executive decision. Alexis had put her in charge of this contest, after all.

Sofia held up the letter. "Guess what? We have a grand-prize winner."

And without another thought, she picked up the phone and dialed the number on the entry.

Boone Dalton's phone buzzed in the pocket of his leather jacket, and he let it go to voice mail. Not that he ever listened to his messages. Who did that? His parents, probably. Not him. He'd just take a look at caller ID and return the call when he got the chance.

He led Nugget, the quarter horse he'd been training, back to the stables.

"You did good today, girl. I don't know why they claim you're trouble."

At the sound of a bark, he looked down at the white dog with a brown spot over one eye. The dog had just shown up on the ranch a week ago and had taken to following Boone around.

"You, too, of course. Whatever your real name is."

The dog yipped and yapped again, and Boone bent down to give him a quick pat. "Suppose if you stick around here much longer, I might have to give you a name."

When his father won big at the gambling tables in Las Vegas, the family had moved to Bronco. He'd then bought Dalton's Grange, giving Boone the opportunity to follow his dream of training horses. He'd been riding since he was four, and his mother often accused him of liking horses more than he did people. Which wasn't exactly true.

The only people he didn't like were the Abernathys and Taylors of Bronco Heights. The kind of people who believed that because they'd had their money longer, and had a so-called legacy, this made them better than anyone else. So far, they hadn't even accepted the Daltons into The Association.

Well, he had news for them. People weren't bred for good stock like horses and dogs. People were people, whether they had money or nothing at all. He'd been on both sides now. Growing up middle-class meant that he still didn't relate to someone who would take a helicopter to go grab lunch in Missoula.

Boone handed the horse over to one of the ranch hands, cleaned up and pulled his phone out to see about that call from earlier. He didn't recognize the number. They'd probably dialed wrong, but he called back anyway.

"BH Couture, this is Sofia Sanchez. How can I help you?"

BH Cou-what? "Well, Sofia, this is Boone Dalton. I have a missed call from y'all, but I think you must have dialed wrong. Just thought I'd let you know. You might want to take another look at that number."

"Oh, no, Mr. Dalton! It isn't a mistake."

"Do I know you?" He'd never even stepped foot inside a couture, whatever that was.

She laughed. "You won the grand prize! A make-over, and wardrobe from our new men's designer line. Your entry stood out above all the others and sincerely spoke to me. When can you come in so that we can start the styling process? I'm very excited to work with you."

"Um, *what*?"

"I have some time tomorrow. About seven?"

"Wait. What do you mean by *styling* process?" Boone was beginning to smell a rat.

"I'm a fashion stylist, and that's what I do. I'll

be working with you to find you the ideal wardrobe from our new men's line."

Aha. Suddenly everything fell into place. Last week his two younger brothers, Dale and Shep, had mentioned that Boone might want to start dressing better if he ever wanted to get a girl. But he did just fine with the ladies, thank you. If a woman wanted fancy-schmancy, she could go after the Taylors and Abernathys of this world. The "suits." He wanted someone real, anyway. A woman who wouldn't care about that sort of stuff and wouldn't judge him the way everyone else in town seemed to.

No doubt, Thing 1 and Thing 2 had entered him into this contest as one of their many practical jokes. Last month they'd set up a fake profile for him on Tinder in which they'd written that he loved "walking in the rain and warm snuggles in front of a fireplace."

Now Boone was going to have to explain this, and excuse his brothers' lame joke because he didn't either want or need a makeover. Besides, the minute this woman found out that he hadn't even entered the contest, he'd be disqualified. Either way, he owed her an apology in person for having wasted her time. Besides, she sounded sweet, like she honestly wanted to help. It wasn't her fault his brothers were idiots.

So he said, "Sure, I'll see you tomorrow."

Hanging up, he headed from the stables to the

sprawling luxe ranch house where his parents and younger brothers lived. He ran up the stone steps, threw open the ten-foot doors and stomped through the entry that still reminded him of the lobby of a ski resort.

"Dale! Shep! What did you two bozos do now?"

Chapter Two

The next evening, Boone pulled into the parking lot of BH Couture. Even if he'd been somewhat intrigued by the sound of the sweet voice on the other end of the phone, he wasn't here to be friendly. He was here to explain Thing 1 and Thing 2's latest practical joke and tell Sofia she'd have to pick someone else. Naturally, he'd apologize profusely, because his mother had raised him to be a gentleman.

Boone opened the doors and strolled inside. Not surprisingly, even the air in here smelled stuck-up. The scent was flowery, just like the perfume that his father had bought his mother recently. It was just one of the many "I love you" gestures that Neal gave Deborah on a weekly, if not daily, basis.

There were racks of clothing lining every wall, and what appeared to be hundreds of shoes. Both male and female headless mannequins were dressed in fancy duds. A large triple mirror stood in the back, in front of a white couch. A woman turned to him, and when she did, Boone stopped processing thoughts.

She was *stunning*. Long, straight red hair, shimmering eyes the color of milk chocolate. He'd pictured a cute and sweet girl on the other end of the line, not…this. Boone might not be a big fan of fashion, but he appreciated the way the blue dress she wore accentuated every one of her curves. He couldn't stop staring.

"Welcome! I'm Sofia, how can I help you?"

Boone gulped. "You're Sofia?"

"Yes." She strutted in his direction and stopped a few feet from him.

"I'm Boone Dalton."

She blinked and her head swiveled as if in surprise. That double take made him run a hand through his hair. He should have brushed it before coming inside. His mother tried to remind him daily that he should care a little more about his appearance. And for the first time in a long while, he did.

"B-Boone? You're a little early. I'm sorry. You caught me off guard."

"Yeah, I should explain. See, the thing is…" He really should tell her the truth, but maybe after he'd had a chance to get her phone number. "Um, I've never done anything like this before."

The words were out of his mouth before he could stop himself. Surely it wouldn't do any harm. Obviously, *someone* had to win this contest.

She cocked her head, a sympathetic look in her eyes. "I bet. There's a first time for everything. Right?"

She smiled, and that was some smile. Boone literally felt his heart rate kick up. His older brother Morgan had talked about feeling electrically zapped with a live wire when he'd met Erica, who was now his wife. Wonder if this was what he'd meant.

"Yeah. Guess you're right."

"Right this way, Boone. Any relation to Daniel?" She winked.

"Huh? Oh, no. Not that I know about."

She leaned in and lowered her voice to a whisper. "Just so you know, my brothers could never afford to come in here, either. Heck, if I didn't work here, I couldn't afford to step inside."

Boone froze. She must think he was poor, and why not? Dale and Shep had entered him into a contest as if he couldn't afford to pay for a brand-new wardrobe ten times over. From here, she couldn't see Dalton's Grange, nor the sprawling ranch house his parents lived in. She didn't know they owned enough horses and cattle to pay for this entire building many times over. Now maybe he could just be Boone Dalton again, the man he was before all this new family wealth complicated his life.

If she liked him at all, it would be because of who he was and not what he had.

Sofia led Boone toward the back of the store. Lori, one of their salesclerks, walked by, giving Boone the side-eye. It was complete disapproval at his ultra-casual look, but he didn't even seem to notice. Ob-

viously, she saw someone from Bronco Valley and
had already made her judgments.

"Right this way, Mr. Grand-Prize Winner," Sofia
said, loudly enough for Lori to overhear.

Hey now, no being rude to our winner, missy.

The way Boone dressed met every one of her defi-
nitions of a hardworking cowboy. Tan, lightly wind-
burned skin. She could almost picture him out on the
range, in the sun, riding his trusty horse. Not like Jordan Taylor, the wealthy cattle rancher that her sister
Camilla had married. Boone was the kind of cowboy the Taylors hired to do the backbreaking work.

His jeans were worn and faded, and boots a little
scuffed. But none of that detracted from his staggering good looks. His wavy brown hair was naturally
tousled. Her hairstylist mother, Denise, purposely
achieved this mussed, strategically disheveled look
for her male clientele, and they paid her well for
it. Boone's deep blue eyes shimmered with intel-
ligence and…something else. Kindness, Sofia decided. Rangy and leanly muscled, he looked like a
man who spent most of his time outdoors. But rather
than smell like he worked outside, his scent was of
leather and Ivory soap.

*Back to work, Sofia. No drooling over Mr. Grand-
Prize Winner.*

She picked up the tablet from the end table next
to the couch. "I just have a few key questions to give
me some idea of your natural style."

"My style? You're lookin' at it." He grinned, and a single dimple flashed.

Hoo boy. Sofia had a thing for dimples. "Well, this is your working style, isn't it? I mean, I'm sure you just got off a hard day working on a ranch."

"Um, yeah." He tipped back on his heels. "I'm a horse wrangler by trade, but I dress this way all the time."

She quirked a brow. "Sure, but now that you'll have a nice sparkling new designer men's wardrobe, you'll have more…options."

"If you say so."

"Surely there are weddings to attend. Dates with the ladies. Holiday parties, that kind of thing."

For instance, the upcoming Taylor-Cruise wedding. But this poor guy probably *worked* for the Taylors or Abernathys. She imagined, dressed as he was, that he rarely came off the ranch. And he was a horse wrangler. How interesting. She didn't know too much about that line of work, but one would think patience would be required. Patience and kindness.

"I don't get invited to much." He shrugged.

Those words hit her heart with a swift kick, but he didn't look particularly disturbed by his lack of social connections.

"That will change once you spend some time with me."

"Oh yeah?" He slid her a flirtatious, slow and easy smile.

She realized she'd sounded a bit too personal and clutched the tablet to her chest. "I mean, after I style you. You're bound to get plenty of invites to parties. Maybe even a date or two."

"That's what I'm hoping."

He took a seat on the couch, leaning back and spreading his legs in that way guys did to claim their space and exert their absolute command over it. If she read him right, he was an alpha male who needed dark colors and sleek lines. He would be transformed with the wardrobe she envisioned. Move over, Henry Cavill. Oh, yasss!

"Okay, I have a few questions to ask before I decide what perfect pieces I can put together for your new wardrobe. Answer with the first thing that comes to mind." She sat down and started on her premade list. "Favorite color?"

"Blue."

Like your eyes. "Favorite season?"

"I'd have to say summer. So far, this test is way too easy. When are you going to start with the hardballs?"

"This is *not* a test, but all right, you asked for it. Favorite movie hero?"

He seemed stumped by this question, as he drummed his fingers on his thigh. "Such weird questions. Kevin Costner."

"That makes sense. He has acted in several Westerns."

"What's with all these questions?"

"This helps give me an idea of who you are."

He slid her a slow grin. "All you have to do is spend time with me, and you'll know."

"Isn't that what we're doing here?" She asked him a few more questions, which he answered, some with an eye roll.

When Sofia closed the tablet and rose, he also stood.

"That's it?"

"Oh, hardly! This is just the beginning." She pulled out her cloth tape measure. "Of course, I'll… need your measurements."

He gave her a steady, deliberate look that made her stomach quiver. What in the world was wrong with her? He was just a *guy*. She dated all the time. Boone was certainly a different kind of man from the type who usually asked her out, but this was no big deal. So *what*? He was good-looking. Stop the presses.

"You can keep your clothes on, of course." No sooner had the words come out of her mouth than she wanted to smack her forehead.

"Good, because you have to buy me dinner before I take my shirt off." He casually shrugged out of his leather jacket and set it down.

Gulp. There went that slow grin, and Sofia reminded herself she was at work. "Don't worry, I'm a professional."

She wasn't going to lie; saying it out loud helped. It was a reminder to herself. Taking a deep breath, she measured the inseam of his arm and the width of his shoulders across his flannel shirt.

"Don't you need to write this down?"

"I'll remember." Geez, would she remember. These were healthy shoulders. Nice and wide. And long, muscular arms, big, callused hands.

Clearing her throat, she stepped much closer to measure his waist, which earned her another slow smile.

"Okay. Got the waist." Sofia decided to get his pant inseam at another time. Or never.

"How much longer are we going to be?" Boone said. "I'm starved."

"Almost done here."

"Why don't we continue this over dinner?"

"Dinner?"

Was he asking her out? Like on a *date*?

"It's that thing when two people sit down and eat food together," he replied.

Okay, so he was a smart-ass. She almost smiled. "Well, I'm…"

"Look, I'm not trying to put the moves on you if that's what you're worried about. It was an early day for me, and I didn't have time to stop for lunch. I'll need to grab something for dinner before I can answer any more of your probing questions."

"It's just that I'm off in a few minutes. I was going to stay late for you, but…"

"Even better. We can do this on my own dime. I'll pay for dinner."

"No, I couldn't let you do that!" With the way he looked, she should pay for *his* dinner.

"Don't you want to get to know the real me?" He winked. "You haven't even asked me about my favorite food."

"It's not on my list."

"Well, it should be. Don't you think what people like to eat tells you something about them?"

Sofia agreed, just not anything having to do with couture. But it was a thought. "Well, I did skip lunch."

"Perfect. You can quiz me over dinner."

Sofia decided that she had to eat anyway, so even though she had leftover chicken at home from the Library, the restaurant her sister Camilla owned, she'd treat this hardworking cowboy to a nice meal.

"Okay, then I'll buy you dinner." *And then you can take your shirt off.*

"No way. It was my idea, after all."

Sofia didn't know how to argue the point. He might be insulted if she didn't think he could afford to buy her dinner. She'd just have to think of a reasonably priced place to eat.

"I'll get my coat."

In fact, Alexis had been bugging her to try the hooded Toscana sheepskin coat. They were often sent samples by new designers and Sofia was a standard size 6, the size designers sent. By the time she'd grabbed the beautiful coat and her purse and said her goodbyes, Boone was waiting for her just outside the entrance.

He opened it for her as he saw her approach. "Ready?"

Outside, the clear Montana night enveloped them with its usual spray of bright stars against a black-velvet sky. No snow was forecast, but the light wind was cold and biting.

"How about DJ's Deluxe?" Boone asked as he hooked a thumb in that direction.

Though DJ's Deluxe was within walking distance, it was on the expensive side. Maybe she could talk him into going dutch.

"My sister used to work there before she opened up her own restaurant."

"Would you rather go there?"

"No. That's fine. I'd like to walk if that's okay with you."

"Sure." They walked side by side in silence for a few seconds. "That's a nice coat," he finally said as he cast her a side glance.

"It's not mine. I get to try some of the samples the designers send. I could never afford this one on my own."

"Why? How much is it?"

"Oh, you don't want to know. These designers set crazy prizes that only wealthy people can afford."

"Yeah."

Probably her imagination, but he cleared his throat and seemed a little uncomfortable as he stuck his hands in the pockets of his jacket and bent his head. Damn, had she managed to make him feel worse? She wanted him to know that despite the fact that she had some wealthy friends (and now relatives), she was part of the working class, too.

"Usually we would need reservations at DJ's Deluxe, but since it's a weeknight we should be fine," Sofia said. "If not, we can sit at the bar."

"You still haven't asked me my favorite food."

"Right. Okay, what's your favorite food?"

"A juicy, flame-broiled burger. But you will never hear me say no to barbecue anything. I'm a simple guy."

"Noted."

Inside, DJ's Deluxe was slammed for a weeknight, but they were able to secure a couple of bar stools.

"Don't worry," she told him, "they serve the full menu here."

Until she sat down, Sofia hadn't realized that Boone stood right behind her. He helped her off with her coat.

"Do you want me to see about checking it?" Boone leaned in close, his breath tickling her neck, which sent a tingle down her spine.

The coat was worth more than one month's rent. She'd be too afraid to lose it. "No, I'll just keep it with me. Thanks."

Boone took a seat on the stool next to her, his knee bumping hers. "I guess you've been here plenty of times since your sister used to work here?"

"Oh, sure. I know DJ and his wife, Allaire. They live in Thunder Canyon, but he comes up often to check on the business. Allaire came up for a visit this time, too."

"Just stick with you and I might get in on a Saturday night sometime?" He grinned.

My goodness, that dimple! "Maybe. I don't like to pull any favors, though."

"I've been here before with my…" He hesitated. "Brothers."

"How many brothers do you have?"

"Four of them. It's cruel. Two older and two younger. Thing 1 and Thing 2 are the youngest."

She laughed. "So you're the middle child. No sisters?"

"Nope." He shook his head and grinned. "My poor sainted mother."

"I'm sure she loves being surrounded by her adoring boys."

He snorted. "That's one way to put it. At least now she has a couple of daughters-in-law."

"We both have large families. There are five of us, too. I have Camilla, that's my sister, then my three brothers. Felix, Dylan and Dante, who are all older."

She paused, wondering how much more she should tell him about Camilla. She was now married to a multimillionaire, Jordan Taylor of Taylor Beef. Probably not someone that Boone would know personally, but there was no way a Bronco resident would not have heard of Taylor Beef. Especially not a cowboy. Still, Sofia didn't want to sound like a name-dropper.

She redirected the conversation to her parents and something he might relate to. "My father, Aaron, works for the post office. He says since he's delivered the mail in this town for years and years, he knows everyone's secrets."

Boone's neck swiveled back, and was that concern she saw flicker in his eyes? Hmm.

What do you have to hide, Mr. Grand Prize?

"He's just kidding, of course," she quickly added to put him at ease. "And my mom, Denise, is a hair-stylist."

"Style runs in the family."

Sofia couldn't resist, and her fingers, almost independent from her brain, reached to rumple Boone's hair. "You have no idea how much men pay for hair like yours."

Yep, just as she thought. Not an ounce of hair spray or gel on that hair. But she regretted satisfying her curiosity a moment later. The casual gesture suddenly felt far too intimate. Boone's eyes smoldered with heat, and tension spread between them heavy and thick.

"What's so great about my hair?"

She swallowed and busied herself with studying the menu she knew by heart. "It's adorably tousled."

"It's called the wind, and I'm not wearing my hat."

"Regardless, men ask my mom for this style all the time. It's usually achieved with plenty of hair spray and gel to make sure it doesn't go anywhere."

She would have said more, but he was studying her with hooded eyes, and she thought food was a safer subject than his hair.

"All right. What are you having?" she asked, breaking eye contact. "I highly recommend the potato skins."

"I haven't tried those yet. I'm a burger and domestic beer kind of guy."

"And I agree. The simple things are often the best." She flipped through the menu, trying to distract herself from the giddy sense of being on a date with her new crush.

Hold up. This was *not* a date. Just two new friends having dinner together because they both happened to be hungry. He was the winner of the contest, her client, and she refused to be unprofessional. This meant that even though she couldn't stop noticing his smoldering hot looks, this would have absolutely no effect on her whatsoever.

"I… I think I'm going to have the potatoes…hot potatoes," Sofia said, risking another look at that sexy beard bristle on his jaw.

"*Hot* potatoes? Aren't they always hot?" Boone slid her a grin.

"Um, what?" Sofia straightened. Too much reflecting on the hot cowboy next to her. "I meant the potato skins. Yes, of course, they're hot, too. You know what, I always have those. I'm having a burger tonight." She shut the menu.

"Why don't we get potato skins as an appetizer and we can share them?"

But this night was going to cost him more than she'd intended. The last thing he needed was a big restaurant bill. Maybe she should switch her order to a simple garden salad.

"Are you sure? I mean, I don't have the room for all that food."

He winked. "I assure you, I have enough room for the both of us."

"Maybe I should just have a garden salad instead," she offered.

"Have the burger. That's what you want."

"Um, okay, then."

She hoped that he had a bigger food allowance than he did a clothing one.

Chapter Three

Boone forced his attention to the menu. It dawned on him that Sofia obviously didn't think he could afford a place like DJ's. Boone had been in here plenty of times before with his brothers. Unfortunately, the last time he'd had a few too many beers and nearly started a fistfight. Some rancher type had muttered "lowlife" in Shep's direction. Boone didn't care what anyone said of him, but no one would talk to his brother like that.

Unfortunately, his tendency to be a little rough around the edges was the least of his problems at the moment. Sofia clearly believed him to be someone's ranch hand, not a landowner. Truthfully, even though Dalton's Grange belonged to his family, he'd only moved to Bronco because his mother asked him to. He'd have been happy to continue living in Whitehorn. Back there, Boone knew when a woman liked him. Now, every woman he met seemed to know all about Dalton's Grange, and ordered every expensive item off the menu.

But then again, it was entirely possible that Sofia

hadn't yet made the connection to him and Dalton's Grange. Possibly due to the sad letter his brothers had written that had apparently made him sound like a street urchin.

As they lingered over their burgers and beers, Sofia told him about her family. They were obviously a close bunch, having a big dinner together every Sunday. Growing up, Boone's family had done the same. But in recent years, Boone hadn't joined them, and he tended to treat Neal as more of an employer than a father.

"You're close to your family. It's nice to see," Boone said. "Not everyone can say the same."

"How about you?"

"I'm close to my mother. And to my brothers, even if the two younger ones are a couple of bozos."

"Bozos?" She scrunched up her adorable nose.

"We're always playing practical jokes on each other. But they seem to have way more time on their hands than I do. Last week, they set up a fake Tinder profile for me."

Sofia laughed. "You're not the online dating type, then?"

"Nope. Are you?"

"Are you *kidding* me? My father would kill me if I tried that, and if he didn't, my brothers would. I'm supposed to meet someone the old-fashioned way." She pulled out her phone. "But I'm pretty active on social media. I have to be, for my career."

"That's another thing I don't do."

"You're kind of old school for someone so young."

Boone shook his head and pulled his phone out from his jacket. "Don't have great Wi-Fi on the ranch anyway. If it helps, I give great text."

If she caught the play on words, she gave him no clue. "Good to know."

"Here." He reached for her phone and sent himself a text. "Now you have me in your phone. Text me anytime."

"Okay, cowboy." She had a sweet smile that lit up her entire face.

Boone hadn't missed the fact that almost every guy here had his eye on her the moment they'd walked in. She'd waved to quite a few people, who all waved back. Sofia carried herself with the air and sophistication of a confident woman. Boone admired her self-assurance, and he'd bet she moved seamlessly between her two worlds.

"You must work with a lot of wealthy people at the store," Boone said carefully.

He wondered what the odds were that she'd styled his sister-in-law, Erica Abernathy Dalton.

"Yes, that's true." She seemed thoughtful. "I think Jessica Taylor has us on speed dial."

Cornelius Taylor's fourth, or was that his fifth, wife? He defined everything Boone detested about this town. Say what you will about Neal, but though he'd cheated on Boone's mother, he'd wised up. He claimed to love his wife, and Boone wanted to believe it, but he'd probably never forgive his old man for his indiscretions and the agony he'd caused his mother.

"Actually, my sister is married to Jordan Taylor, Cornelius's son." She took a pull of her beer and set it down. "And I know what you're thinking, but Jordan…he's different."

Good thing he hadn't said more about Cornelius. But he also thought Erica was special, both to Morgan and their family, so maybe there was some truth to her words. Not everyone was tainted by their family, he supposed.

"My family is still pretty new to Bronco, and maybe because of that, it feels like we're not as accepted by some."

"You all moved here together?"

"I didn't want to leave Whitehorn, but my mother begged all of us brothers to come along. We were scattered all over Montana at the time. This is like a new start for all of us. She had a heart attack, and I guess she realizes how fragile the time we have together is. Me, too. I don't know how much longer she'll be around."

"Oh, Boone. I'm sorry."

"It's all good. She's fully recovered. But her heart attack made us all realize we're a family, and we always will be."

Even if sometimes he wished to cut dear old

dad out of the picture. Neal Dalton didn't deserve Deborah's forgiveness. His unfaithfulness wasn't a "slipup," as she referred to it. He didn't put a *shoe* on the wrong foot. But Boone didn't need to lay all his family dysfunction on Sofia.

After dinner, Boone paid, and they walked the two blocks back to the store.

"Thank you for dinner," she said, her hand on the lapel of her luxurious coat. "We can start on your makeover tomorrow. How's that?"

"Sure, I'll swing by around the same time."

She clicked her keys to unlock her economy sedan, and he swung the door open for her.

Boone waited until she drove away before he walked to his own fully loaded, brand-spanking-new Land Rover. Climbing in, he pulled out his phone and sent her a quick text, replying to the one he'd sent himself from her phone:

Hey, it's me, the one with great text. See you tomorrow.

The next morning, Boone walked over from his cabin on Dalton's Grange to check in on his mother. He had a long day ahead, going through the paces with Nugget, making sure she'd be ready for her owner, a fifteen-year-old girl who barrel-raced competitively.

The crisp Montana air lifted his spirits on his

walk, as did the thought he'd be seeing Sofia again tonight. When he'd gotten home last night she'd texted him back:

You're right. You give great text. Thank you again for dinner.

She added a burger emoticon, followed by a yummy emoticon, followed by a happy face.

He'd never met a woman quite like her, someone who seemed just as comfortable in her own skin with a poor ranch hand as with an Abernathy type. Even though her sister was married to Jordan Taylor, Boone didn't get the feeling that Sofia wanted her own millionaire. Otherwise, why waste her time with him?

Then again, last night hadn't been a date, even with all the flirting. He'd have to find out first if she'd date him without knowing about all his money. Today or tomorrow, he'd tell her about his brothers entering this contest for him. It didn't feel right to keep that from her, but what if she then wanted to choose someone else? Not having entered on his own would disqualify him.

He found his mother in the spacious kitchen with exposed wood beams, looking out the window at their expansive view of the Montana skyline. The fireplace that separated the kitchen from the great room roared with a warm fire. A nice image, and

Boone's heart swelled because his mother finally had the home of her dreams. She deserved it and then some.

"Hey, honey." She turned to him, a mug in her hands.

"I hope that's decaf." He pointed to her cup before he bussed her cheek.

"Decaf herbal tea," she said with a smile. "What's on your agenda today?"

"Still working with the quarter horse. She goes back in a few days."

"Do you want me to cook you a nice breakfast? Your father and I already ate."

"Nah, I don't have time for that. Just wanted to pop in and say hi." Still, he grabbed a muffin from the basket on the granite counter.

Dale blew in then, smelling fresh off mucking stalls. "Hey, Mr. Grand Prize."

"And there's the *other* reason I'm here," Boone said. "I need to thank my brothers for entering me in a contest I didn't know existed and wouldn't have wanted to win even if I had."

"What did you do now, Dale?" his mother said, hand on her hip.

Dale looked suddenly uncomfortable under their mother's scrutiny, and before he could even open his mouth, Boone told her. "They entered me to win a makeover at BH Couture and a designer wardrobe."

"Dale! What does Boone need with that?"

"He doesn't have to take the makeover, though he sure could use it," Dale quipped, washing his hands at the sink. "When's the last time you got a new pair of boots, anyway?"

"What's the big deal? Every time they get too worn, I buy new ones. I can only wear one pair at a time. But he's right, Mom. I think I need a make-over."

Dale howled. "You're going through with this?"

"I should thank you idiots. You introduced me to the most beautiful woman I've ever met. I think I'll be the one having the last laugh here."

"You're welcome," Dale said.

"How wonderful, Boone," his mother said. "I've always said you look so handsome in a suit."

"When have you ever seen in him in a suit?" Dale asked.

"Let me think. I guess it was Morgan's wedding?"

Boone held up a hand. "Don't remind me. That wasn't a suit. I felt like a penguin."

All three were laughing when their father strolled into the kitchen and went right up to his wife. He set her mug down and pulled her into his arms. "Good morning, my angel."

"You already said good morning, sweetheart."

"Well, it's still a good morning, isn't it?" He kissed her, for a little too long, in Boone's opinion.

Boone exchanged a look with Dale. Secretly, they both believed Neal should drop to his knees every morning before Deborah. But she seemed happy, so they were all trying to accept the fact that their parents were behaving like newlyweds.

"I better get going." Boone strode through the kitchen toward the glass-and-wood-paned doors of the wraparound deck.

He was all the way down the steps when Neal called out to him. "Boone!"

Boone stopped but didn't turn around. "What?"

Neal ran down the rest of the steps to meet him. "Are you always going to bolt from the room when I walk in?"

Boone turned slowly. "Don't make this about you. I have a lot of work today."

"You boys are going to have to come around sooner or later. Your mother forgave me. Holt and Morgan, too. Why can't you?"

He made it sound like he'd accidentally stepped on her foot. Boone spoke through his tight jaw. "I'm working on it."

"Maybe you want to try talking to me sometime, like a son. I'd like you to be an example to Dale and Shep. They both look up to you. While they're still living at the main house, I have a real chance to get them to forgive me also, and we can all move on."

Yeah, Boone thought. And then Neal could come out looking like the good guy, all shiny and bright.

He'd gambled, and that one time, it paid off big.

Never mind all the times he drank too much, stayed out all night and lost money at the tables.

Boone remembered those nights, when his mother looked worried and worn out. When Boone would catch her waiting up late for Neal, glancing at her watch, sometimes waiting by the phone. His father screwed up, time and again—yet his mother would always take him back.

"Look, I appreciate everything you've done for Mom and continue to do. Just keep it up. She's obviously forgiven you, and as long as she's happy, I'm happy." He started on his way, till his father's comment made him turn back.

"I wish it were that simple."

For the first time in ages, Boone took a good long look and realized that Neal Dalton looked whipped, the lines around his eyes deeper than last year, and Boone almost felt a tug of sympathy. Then he remembered his mother's heart attack and the sympathy fled.

"I want to do something for each of you boys," Neal told him. "Something to make up for everything I've put you all through. It wasn't just your mother I let down."

"Thanks, but I don't need anything else. This ranch and the work I can do here is enough."

"There has to be something else. Some way I can help get your name out as a top horse wrangler.

Maybe there's some kind of business angle here I'm not seeing yet."

Just like his father to look at ways of raking in even more money. He just didn't get it, and Boone had no more patience for this conversation. "I've got a horse to train, so I better get going."

"Fine, son. You go on ahead. I'm proud of you. Folks are saying you're the best horseman they've ever seen. The horse whisperer of Bronco, they say."

And here Boone thought *he* was the only one who called himself that. Good to know that after two years of being in this town he was getting some respect—as a horseman, if nothing else.

At the end of the day, Boone could hardly wait to shower, change and head over to see Sofia for his makeover. He understood this meant he'd be trying on clothes he'd probably never want to wear except to a wedding or a funeral, but it might be good to stretch himself. His mother certainly liked to see him dressed up. And all this was a small price to pay for spending time with Sofia.

When he strolled in the shop, he was greeted by a blonde woman he'd seen the night before. "I'm Alexis, the owner. Congratulations on winning our grand prize."

"Thanks, I really appreciate it."

"I read your entry, too." She went hand to heart. "*So* touching."

Lord, what *had* his brothers written about him? They must have piled it on thick. He should have thought to ask.

"Well, um, thanks. That…means a lot to me."

"Well, come right this way," she said as she led him to the rear of the shop. "Sofia has been hard at work designing an amazing wardrobe for you. You'll see. She has a sense of style like no one else."

Sofia turned as he approached and gave him a wide smile. She wore a short brown-and-white dress that showed off her long legs. The tan ankle boots she wore emphasized the curve of her calves. She looked so tempting, he nearly swallowed his tongue.

"Hi, Boone!" She held up a dark jacket on a hanger. "I've got the most amazing wardrobe picked out for you."

"Uh…that's great!" he said weakly. "Can I see if I like it first?"

"Of course. In the end the choices will all be yours. As long as you agree to move beyond denim and leather," she teased. "And I had to guess your pant length because I…forgot to get your inseam, but getting the right size is a special gift of mine."

"Okay." Boone shrugged out of his jacket. "Just pretend I'm a life-size mannequin."

He noticed some of the clothes she'd laid out. Everything looked uncomfortable. Scratchy. He'd bet that they would itch when he put them on, bringing back memories of Easter Sundays as a child, when he didn't have a choice of what he wore to church.

"What's wrong?"

Great. She'd noticed the scowl on his face. He forced himself to smile. "Um, nothing. Just looking forward to this."

"Don't be afraid." She laughed. "The shirt is *silk*. It will feel soft against your skin."

Damn, she'd read his mind. Sorry, but he didn't believe for a second that silk would feel as soft as her hands on him.

"Don't worry, I trust you."

"Good, because I'm not going to make you suffer for the sake of fashion."

She slipped the shirt off its hanger and then, somewhat shyly, stepped closer. "Do you…um, want to take your shirt off?"

Oh, man, did he ever! He couldn't unbutton and remove his flannel shirt fast enough.

Sofia came close, holding the shirt open for him, and he slid his arm in one sleeve and then the other. He felt odd but couldn't deny that his favorite part of this entire situation was having a beautiful woman dress him. It was an odd statement to be sure, as he hadn't been dressed by anyone since age four.

He'd been about to button up when Sofia, who'd held the shirt behind him, came around to face him.

"Stop moving around so much. Are you always this jittery?"

Only when around a drop-dead gorgeous woman. "Always."

She began to slowly button his shirt and he quickly abandoned all thought of doing it himself. He swallowed at her light flowery scent.

"Yeah. This looks good. Really good." She gave him a slow smile and smoothed down the material at his shoulders.

"I couldn't agree more."

And he wasn't talking about the shirt.

Chapter Four

Sofia couldn't very well pretend Boone was a mannequin when he constantly moved. Nor when touching him was like a feast for her senses. His long arms were lean and sinewy to her touch. Today he smelled like sandalwood and pine. When he looked at her, his warm blue eyes seemed to read her thoughts, and the sound of his deep voice tugged at something inside her she refused to admit.

She was incredibly drawn to him with an unmistakable pull, even though she knew it was supremely unprofessional. She'd never once developed any kind of attraction for a client.

During dinner at DJ's Deluxe, he'd been charming and attentive. Though she dated a lot, handsome men included, she wasn't usually immediately comfortable with a man, not like she was with Boone. Last night, as she'd tried to find sleep, she couldn't stop thinking of him. His family.

The fact that he didn't feel welcome in Bronco even though they'd already been here for two years was obviously an issue for him. Clearly, Boone wasn't really *new* in town, but that they still hadn't found their place. Her heart squeezed tightly at the thought. He didn't need her pity, but instead she found that she commiserated with him.

Sofia liked to fit in, too, and she didn't know anyone who didn't. Even though she was a confident woman, sometimes she worried that her personality wasn't big enough. Sparkly enough. She leaned toward being an introvert, having grown up spending her time drawing and dreaming. So she paid special attention to her looks to make up the difference. It helped that a dress, coat, hairstyle and makeup, in her own unique style, gave her a natural confidence that she didn't have to fake.

Sofia hadn't ever been the cowboy-loving type. Living in Bronco, hot and virile cowboys were all over the place, and she didn't much care for the cliché. Ranchers and cowboys were fine for those who planned to stick around Bronco forever, but Sofia had always thought she should date someone who had aspirations like her own—with a wardrobe to match. She certainly wasn't basing her entire dating life on appearances—but deep down, she was beginning to wonder if she'd been judging too many books by their covers.

Boone came out of the dressing room wearing the black slacks she'd selected, paired with the blue silk shirt that brought out his eyes.

"No offense at that special talent of yours, but I

think you got the wrong size. These are too tight."
He moved one leg and then the next, fidgeting.

"This is a slim-fit suit. They're supposed to fit
that way."

Sofia loved this designer. But even more, she
loved the way Boone filled out those slacks. They
might be uncomfortable, but they showcased his
great butt and strong thighs. Not that she would tell
him that.

"Yeah?" He stretched, looking antsy in his own
skin. He pulled at the collar of his long-sleeved silk
button-down and winced.

"Take my word for it." She stepped close to wind
the patterned silk tie around his neck.

His beautiful, warm neck made her want to bury
her face there and inhale his delicious scent. Instead,
she pulled up the shirt collar and did her magic.
Some men, her brothers included, didn't wear a tie
often enough to know how to put one on the right
way. She'd learned years ago as a teenager by watching YouTube videos. It was a challenge, she supposed, and had certainly come in handy.

"This is my favorite part," Boone said, his voice
husky.

"Putting on a tie?" She wound it through the
loops, trying not to let his eyes affect her. Every
time she looked into them, his hooded, bedroom eyes
made her feel all warm and prickly.

He chuckled. "I hate anything around my neck."

She reached for the blazer nearby and eased it on. It fit like a glove, accentuating those broad shoulders and his incredible physique. She smoothed the material over his shoulders, pretending it needed adjusting. This time, she met Boone's eyes and let the attraction between them click into place.

"Sofia! Oh, my goodness, you've outdone yourself," Alexis said, approaching the rear of the boutique. "You look amazing, Boone."

Alexis came behind Boone and dusted off his shoulders, then straightened out his jacket. She looked at him approvingly in the mirror. "Seriously, you look like a male model."

Sofia bit back a smile when Boone winced. "Well, regardless, I'm a cowboy."

"Here at BH Couture, we like to say *rancher*. It has a nicer ring to it." She came around to face Boone and smoothed down the lapels of his blazer.

The "ring" Alexis referred to was money. Legacy money.

When Alexis gave Boone the approving smile she might give to a particularly good-looking model, Sofia told herself that she was just doing a good job with their winner. Making him feel worthy of this wardrobe. Welcome. Convincing him that he looked good and should wear it.

But it didn't feel that way.

Jealousy burned in the pit of her stomach, because

it seemed that Alexis was making a move on Boone. Right here, in front of everyone, Sofia included.

"I'm not done here," Sofia said. "He has more clothes to try on."

"Let me help you," Alexis said.

Alexis's comment that he looked like a model made him remember that the agreement came with a photo shoot. He wanted to kick his own ass. He should have *never* signed up for this.

The only bright light had been the look on Sofia's face when Alexis boldly put her arms around him. Sofia could not disguise the outrage in her gaze. He'd seen jealousy on a woman, and Sofia was jealous. Maybe this whole thing between them wasn't one-sided, as he'd feared. She held herself to a professional standard of behavior.

Whenever Sofia came close, to smooth his shirt or blazer, the moment felt intimate. She was the most desirable woman he'd ever met, and now he realized that he hadn't imagined the sexual tension between them.

"You know," Alexis said, as she and Sofia swapped out shirts and held them in front of Boone. Classic white? Bone white? Cream? He couldn't even see a difference. "I was just thinking about my billboard idea. I can just picture Boone's handsome face smiling out at all of Bronco Heights wearing a suit. Dressed to kill."

"Um, no thanks."

He could just picture his mug all over town, his lips red, his teeth blackened out, horns on his head. They did not know his brothers! Meeting her eyes, he sent SOS signals to Sofia. She had to know how he'd feel about this. The photo shoot would be tough enough for him to get through. He hated all this attention to his looks and only cared what Sofia thought of him.

"Why not?" Alexis pressed. "You could be the face of our new men's clothing line. Why wouldn't you do it? You're so incredibly handsome, so perfectly proportioned…"

"No, sorry. Absolutely not." Boone pulled on the tie that now felt like a noose around his neck about to hang him. "If that's the deal, then I'll just leave the clothes. You can pick another winner."

"Now, Boone. You have to know I don't want that." Alexis faced him. "Just please…think about it."

From behind him, Sofia stepped out. "Alexis, he already said no."

The shop owner sighed heavily. "Oh, all right. Sorry, I just got all excited when I saw how wonderful you look. These clothes have made a new man out of you."

"I hope not. I liked the old man." With that, he snapped the lapels of his blazer.

He caught Sofia biting her lower lip as if to hold back a smile.

Alexis went back to her paperwork, leaving him with Sofia, and within the next hour or so of torture, Boone had tried on three more outfits. Sofia had picked out a tux, and also a fancy coat for him, something that looked too expensive to ever risk getting dirty at the ranch. He might wear it…someday.

"Same time tomorrow?" Boone asked, having changed back into his jeans and flannel shirt.

"Yeah," Sofia said. "Maybe a little earlier?" When he nodded, she said, "I'll walk you out."

He held the boutique door open for her and they walked out side by side. She'd come out without her coat, and an icy wind kicked up. He put his arm around her, almost unconsciously shielding her from the cold.

"It's chilly."

Today he'd driven his old truck, the one he used to haul hay around the ranch. He told himself it was because he didn't want to show off, but truthfully, he liked knowing that Sofia appreciated him even when she thought he had nothing. Maybe even liked him as more than a friend.

"Is this you?" she said when he stopped at the old green Ranger.

"Yep," he said. He reached into his pocket for the key, then turned back to her. Noticing the uncomfortable look on her face, he asked, "What's up? Are you okay?"

She looked down as she replied, "I should ask

you. Alexis was way too aggressive in there and I'm sorry. She doesn't understand that some people don't appreciate all this attention."

"But you understand me?"

"Yes. It may look like I want attention because of the way I dress, but I'm not a snob."

"Hey, hey, I know that." Almost out of instinct, he reacted by tipping up her chin to meet his gaze. He wanted to reassure her. "I never thought you were."

"I just want you to feel welcome in Bronco, you and your entire family." She then brought his fingers from her chin to her lips and brushed a kiss across his knuckles.

She set him on fire with that one movement.

"I already feel a lot more welcome." He threaded his fingers through hers and lowered their joined hands to his side.

"Boone," she said, biting her lower lip and once again avoiding his eyes. "I'm sorry about something else, too."

"Yeah?" He swallowed.

Even if she told him she was sorry she'd set his house on fire, he'd probably still be staring at her milky skin and smelling that delicious scent of coconut in her hair.

"I hope this isn't unprofessional, but… I like you." She glanced up and smiled a little shyly. "I've never met anyone quite like you. You're so comfortable with who you are, so honest and hardworking."

"Okay, now I'm the sorry one." He let go of her hand to run it through his hair, a nervous habit. "I sort of...lied to you."

She paled. "About what?"

"This contest. I didn't win."

"Sure you did. I picked your entry myself."

"I'm going to need to read that entry someday. It was actually written by my younger brothers. Remember, I told you that they're always playing practical jokes? Well, they thought this would be funny. I don't think they ever imagined I'd go through with this makeover."

Her brows knit, and she looked confused. "But everything in the entry is stuff you've told me yourself. How some people just think they're better than others. How your family hasn't felt welcome."

"All true, but I don't need anyone's pity. I have a little pride."

Not to mention a whole lot of money to ease any hurt feelings he might have. But she didn't have to know that just yet. One reveal at a time.

She was quiet for several minutes, that sweet mouth a straight line, simply studying him. "Why did you take the wardrobe? Why let me fit you with clothes you don't want?"

He shrugged, slowly releasing his guilt. "Because when I walked in and took one look at you, I had to see you again. And I needed a good excuse."

She bit her lower lip as if fighting a smile, then

met his gaze and traced his jawline with the pads of her fingers. He was glad he'd shaved this morning.

"I can't get mad when you say things like that."

"And then there was all the touching you had to do when you helped me with my tie or smoothed the shirt and blazer. That was extra stuff I hadn't even counted on."

"Confession time." Stretching, she put a hand on each of his shoulders. "I don't ever touch a client like I've been touching you."

"You mean they can smooth their own shirts and lace their own ties?" He reached to tuck a stray hair behind her ear.

She shrugged and brought her hands down to grip the front of his leather jacket. "It's more that I'm willing to provide direction and let them learn to do it for themselves. I should have done that with you, but…you're just far too irresistible."

It was all the invitation Boone required. Pulling her close into the circle of his arms, he bent to kiss her lips. Her sweet mouth lived up to its promise. She tasted like sugar with a hint of mint. He took the kiss deeper when she made a little sound in the back of her throat that drove him wild. The cold night around them was no longer a concern. They had enough chemistry to start their own roaring fire. When they came up for air, surprise flashed in her eyes. He felt the same way. There was chemistry, magnetic attraction, and then…there was *this*.

Kind of a crazy and unexpected spell. Boone felt mesmerized.

"I'm not going to sleep well tonight." Boone finally spoke, pressing his forehead to hers.

"That makes two of us."

Chapter Five

Sofia drove home to her little apartment above the Bronco Valley post office in a daze. She'd *kissed* Boone. After a long night of imagining what he might taste like, what his lips would feel like on hers, she had her answer. The kiss had been amazing. Good thing they'd been in public or she might have been tempted to see where else it might lead them.

Learning that he hadn't entered the contest suddenly made a lot of sense. Boone actually seemed too confident to care much about how he dressed. Still, she wished he could see himself through her eyes. His good looks shot into the stratosphere with designer clothes. "Clothes make the man" as the old saying went. But yeah, she'd bet Boone looked just as outstanding wearing *no* clothes at all.

One strange question remained. Why had Winona Cobbs chosen Boone's entry when he obviously didn't want the wardrobe? She'd said, "This is the one you've been looking for" and she'd been so certain of it. Well, Sofia supposed even someone with so-called psychic intuition could have an off day.

Upstairs in her studio apartment, she checked her mail. Funny thing, her father working at the post office and her living above it. Sometimes, if she was home, he'd wave to her from the truck as he left for his deliveries. When she got a chance, she'd have to ask him for the scoop on Boone Dalton. Her father had known about Jordan Taylor before anyone else in her family did. That he was one of *those* Taylors. Camilla, now married to Jordan, had lived in this very apartment before she moved into his cabin on the expansive Taylor Ranch. One of the *bathrooms* in her sister's new home was nearly as large as this entire apartment.

Speaking of Camilla, Sofia hadn't talked to her sister in a few days. Instead of texting, the norm for them, Sofia actually went the old-fashioned way and called her.

"Hey there," Camilla answered the phone.

"Are you and Jordan busy?" It wasn't too late, but with those two, Sofia just never knew.

Ever since they got married, Sofia had missed hanging with her sister. Camilla was pretty much her best friend. Sofia had other friends, but no one she confided in like her big sister, who understood Sofia and always gave the best advice.

"We're not joined at the hip, you know."

"So you say." Sofia snorted. But it certainly seemed that way.

She couldn't remember the last time she and Camilla had done something spur-of-the-moment, like a big shopping trip to the city.

Sofia was happy for Camilla, of course. Just as she was with her other friends who all seemed to be getting engaged, married or pregnant. The latest was her old friend Brandon Taylor and Cassidy Ware. They were engaged and already having a baby. Everyone around her was pairing up for forever after, but Sofia wasn't ready for that kind of commitment. Just the idea of pledging the rest of your life to another person seemed nuts at only twenty-six. She didn't even like to commit to what she'd be wearing from one day to the next. Spontaneity and creativity were key, and marriage snuffed that out lickety-split.

She'd had a plan in place from the moment she graduated from college. Work for a boutique, make contacts, network. Then find a financial backer and start her own clothing design line. She had a book full of sketches, and now that she had a portfolio of work she could take pride in, she'd be approaching Alexis. Sofia valued her opinion; she'd been in the business for a while and had many connections.

Like Camilla, Sofia was ambitious and wanted to have a career. While Camilla was still a newlywed, she seemed to be balancing work and marriage well. For now.

"I think... I met someone," Sofia said, biting her cuticle.

"Who is it? Someone I know?"

"I doubt it. He's a *real* cowboy," Sofia teased.

She liked to say that Jordan wasn't a "real" cowboy, considering he spent much of his time in a boardroom. But running Taylor Beef was important, Sofia understood. It just wasn't hard work, in her opinion, which she tried to keep to herself. More to the point, Jordan didn't dress like a ranch hand.

Which meant he could probably give Boone a few pointers.

"Ha ha. So...what's his name?"

"Boone. He's like us, comes from a large family. All brothers."

"How did you meet him?"

"He had the best entry in the contest at the boutique. It was weird. Winona Cobbs came in to get a dress, and she just pointed to his entry. Just like that!" She snapped her fingers.

"Uh-huh. So, does *Winona* get the credit for this?"

Camilla wasn't as big a believer in intuition as Sofia. "Not *full* credit, because I chose him. But she did direct me right to him, so that's something."

"Just another one of those coincidences."

"I really like him." Sofia took a breath. "He's funny, sweet and..."

The word you're looking for is sexy.

Her sister didn't miss a beat. "Do you think that he could be your type?"

"No way! You know I'm not looking for a guy

right now anyway. I'm totally focused on my designs right now."

Camilla chuckled. "Sounds like you at least found your plus-one to Daphne's wedding, didn't you?"

"Maybe."

Sofia wondered if Boone would be comfortable around some of Bronco's most elite ranchers. Then again, the venue for Daphne Taylor's wedding was Happy Hearts, the animal sanctuary she ran. Daphne had called all the shots with this wedding. No long train or wedding veil for her. Sofia had simply fashion-consulted, at Camilla's request. But Daphne decided that everything BH Couture had to offer in the way of designers wasn't her personal style.

Eventually, Sofia had located a secondhand vintage dress through one of her many connections. Daphne loved it. Sofia couldn't wait to see the look on Cornelius Taylor's face when he saw how decidedly anti-traditional his daughter had gone with her wedding dress.

Camilla's question broke into her thoughts. "When are you bringing him over to Sunday dinner? You know that Papi will need to have final approval. You're his little princess, after all."

"If they loved Jordan, they're going to love Boone. He's just one of the guys. A horse trainer." Sofia waited a beat. "But yes, if tonight was any indication, I'd say a Sunday dinner is in our future."

"Wow, is this serious?"

"Don't be ridiculous. You know me. I date a lot. I'm not going to be tied down anytime soon."

"Famous last words," Camilla teased. "Look what happened to me."

But those weren't simply words to Sofia. She still had a lot of living to do. A trip to New York City's Garment District someday, when she could save up enough money. And of course, her own designer label. Someday. All in good time.

Sofia saw Boone at the boutique every night for the next few days. After, they'd hang out at DJ's De-luxe for a cold beer. Boone started work extremely early in the morning and worked long hours, but she'd hear from him frequently throughout the day via text. He'd let her know whether or not he'd made any progress with a difficult horse. Or ask her what she was doing.

Each night, he'd take home another piece of his new wardrobe. A wool suit, a tux for special occasions, four pairs of patent leather loafers, six pairs of slacks with button-down shirts and a lambswool coat. But every time Boone walked into the store, he wore his old jeans, flannel shirt and leather jacket. They were always clean, but they looked the same every day. No variety.

Another matter that hadn't changed was Alexis droning on and on about the billboard.

The day of the photo shoot, Boone arrived in the

early afternoon as scheduled. He took one look at the photographer set up in the corner, the parasol lighting, and stopped short. It seemed he had to force himself to even walk inside.

"You don't have to look like you're going to the dentist for a root canal," Sofia said as she met him near the door.

"I'm looking forward to this about as much."

Sofia smiled at him and patted his arm. "It will be over before you know it."

Alexis joined them, her enthusiasm and excitement bubbling over. "This is so exciting! We have a wonderful photographer. Don't worry about a thing. You're going to do great."

Boone didn't look convinced as he accepted the first outfit from Sofia. A few minutes later he emerged from the changing room wearing a pair of dark slacks and a gray silk button-down.

The tie was dangling haphazardly around his neck, his dimple flashing. "Can you help? I'm all thumbs."

He was not all thumbs, Sofia had learned. He simply had a preference for her to come close and tie it for him.

Truthfully, so did she. "Come here, you."

"Any more thoughts on the billboard?" Alexis asked as she appeared from behind Boone.

Sofia moaned. "Geez, Alexis."

"What? I figured it's my last chance to ask. This is the last fitting for the wardrobe, isn't it?"

"Yes." Sofia could stretch a dollar until it screamed, but even she couldn't get more out of this.

"Sorry, Alexis," Boone said. "I'm afraid it's still a no."

"Really? You don't even want to take a week and think about it?" Alexis whined.

Sofia could take no more of this. Boone wasn't the showy type, and a billboard would be too "in your face," even for her. She'd been asked to model for designers half a dozen times and refused them all. That wasn't her thing, either. She and Boone were alike in that way, too.

"Why not ask Geoff Burris? He's coming to town in a few weeks for the Mistletoe Rodeo, and I heard he's signed a contract with Taylor Beef," Sofia said. "Maybe he wouldn't mind doing the billboard, too, and being the face of our new men's line."

"Thank you, Sofia. I didn't know that." Alexis turned to Boone with a wide grin. "It helps to know the right people. It doesn't hurt to be in-laws with Jordan Taylor, does it?"

This time Sofia knew it wasn't her imagination when Boone tensed.

When Alexis strutted away, Sofia straightened his tie and asked him point-blank, "Do you have an issue with Jordan?"

"No. I have an issue with Cornelius Taylor."

"Everyone has an issue with Cornelius. He's not a terribly nice man."

"He's one of those people I mentioned that have been…unwelcoming."

She wondered if that meant Boone had experienced Cornelius's condescending attitude firsthand. "Do you work on the Taylor Ranch?"

He cocked his head, smiling with a hint of amusement in his gaze. "Not at all. But I probably could be of service, seeing as I'm one of the best horse wranglers in the area."

"I want to meet some of the horses you train and see you in action." This was her lame attempt at making sure tonight wasn't the last she'd see of Boone Dalton.

He brought her hand to his lips and kissed it. "That's definitely going to happen."

"Are we about ready?" the photographer asked.

"Yes, we are. I mean, he is." Sofia stepped to the side.

For the next few minutes, the photographer took shot after shot of Boone. Wearing a tux, the suit and many of the other clothes. Not only the ones he'd won. Alexis wanted a little bit of everything so she could get her money's worth out of her free male model, Sofia guessed.

"Usually models get paid quite a bit of money for this kind of photo shoot," Sofia told him.

"Really? How do you know?"

"One of my graduation projects at Montana State involved designing an outfit from start to finish and hiring a model for a fashion show. Loads of fun."

"You went to school for this?"

"Oh, yes. I'm more than just a pretty face," she deadpanned, playfully sticking out her tongue as the photographer snapped away.

And for someone who didn't like the attention, Boone moved his body with ease. Sofia could hardly take her eyes off him.

As had become their custom, Boone threw his new clothes in the cab of his truck at the end of the night. Then, hand in hand, he and Sofia walked to DJ's Deluxe for a burger and a beer. It might be the last night of fittings, but Boone wouldn't let it be the last time he saw Sofia.

Finally, he'd managed to put the dreaded photo shoot behind him and didn't feel any worse for the experience.

"Hey, Sofia!" Tonight, they were greeted by DJ Traub himself, waving to them. "Got a booth ready for you."

"I guess they're getting used to us dropping by," Sofia said with a chuckle.

Boone didn't think that was the case. He'd learned that Sofia knew just about everyone and was friendly with them, too. They all seemed to like her, from the diners to the waiters, and to the owner himself.

Boone followed her to the table, thoroughly enjoying the view of those swinging hips. That long, swaying hair. Every man in the place turned to look at least once. Some had to do double takes. Not that he blamed any of them. She always looked so put together, every hair in place.

He honestly wanted to see what she looked like when she was pared down to the bare essentials. Nothing but skin and curves. Something told him she'd be even more beautiful, because that beauty of hers wasn't just on the outside, as with so many women he'd dated.

"DJ, this is Boone Dalton," Sofia introduced them. "Boone, meet DJ Traub."

"Yeah, I think I've seen you and your brothers here before." DJ nodded as they shook hands.

"You have the best burgers in Bronco," Boone said as he pulled his chair closer to Sofia's.

"Well, thanks, my man. I love to hear that. I'll send your server over."

"He's a nice man," Sofia said, reaching for Boone's hand after the owner walked away.

He liked the way she took every opportunity to touch him, always keeping contact. A hand on his shoulder, his hand, arm, cheek, chin. And he made it easy for her by staying close. The first time he'd drawn their chairs this close together, she'd chuckled. When he'd asked what was so funny, she'd simply laid her head on his shoulder.

"I have to ask you something," she said now as she fiddled with the silverware. "Would you be my plus-one at the Taylor-Cruise wedding this Saturday?"

"Absolutely," he said without reservation. He'd go, even if forced to wear a tux. "Black tie, I assume?"

"You'd assume wrong. This is Daphne Taylor's wedding, and it's going to be at Happy Hearts, her animal sanctuary."

He squeezed her hand. "This is my kind of wedding! Come as you are."

"It's not that casual. You'll want to wear nice slacks. A tie. Just think, you've got this great new wardrobe. Your first place to use it, too."

"I still feel guilty about that."

Someone else should have that wardrobe, someone who truly couldn't afford it. He could afford this wardrobe many times over with the ridiculously generous salary his father insisted on paying him. He paid all the brothers a salary to run the place. The way Neal said it, Dalton's Grange was their inheritance anyway. And if he kept his sons in charge, there was no way he'd ever lose it.

"Even if your brothers were the ones who entered you, I feel like you deserved to win. It just feels right, you know?" She ruffled his hair. "And I got to spend all this time with you."

"Ditto."

"Did I ever tell you that Winona Cobbs actually pointed me to your entry? 'That's the right one,' she said. At first, I didn't take her seriously, but she does have that psychic booth inside Bronco Ghost Tours. She's been right about a lot of things, I've heard, and she was right about you."

"Do you believe in that sort of thing?" Normally Boone didn't, but he was beginning to believe in destiny.

Hell, he realized it sounded corny. But what a story to tell his grandkids, if he got that lucky.

Your grandmother and I met when my brothers entered me into a contest, and she picked my entry.

Yeah, yeah, okay, he was getting way ahead of himself. And eventually, he would have to tell Sofia the truth. He was one of "those" Daltons. The "rough around the edges" ranchers who had come by their money in one of the least reputable ways: casino gambling. But no matter *where* or how his old man got the money, now he was at least trying to make things right by his family. Trying to give them all a legacy for future generations. Boone had to give him that, even if he gave him nothing else.

He and his brothers were determined that Dalton's Grange would be a successful cattle ranch. It would always remain in the hands of a Dalton. They were making their own legacy.

"I do believe, a little bit. I'm not sure what to call it, but it's more like intuition for me. Like the moment I know I've made a good decision and have zero doubts. The moment I feel truly inspired and the sketch I draw just comes out right in the first draft. Kismet."

"Sketches? You're an artist, too?"

She shrugged, and her cheeks pinkened a little. "Just of clothes. I'm a fashion designer. I have an entire sketchbook filled with my own designs. And my sister helped me put together a business plan."

She reached in her tote bag, pulled out a book and handed it to him. "Someday, I hope to have my own line of clothing."

"Seriously? For women or men?"

He paged through the book, and though he knew little about fashion, her designs looked similar to the clothes he'd seen women buying at the boutique. Even better.

"Well, both I hope. I'll start with women and later branch out." She took a pull of her beer. "My dream is to make beautiful designer fashion affordable for everyone. That's not going to be easy, I know. I'll need to go to New York City and maybe make some contacts there in the garment industry."

"You're moving to New York City?" Boone nearly had heart failure.

Sofia laughed. "No, Bronco is my home and always will be. But I'd like to spend some time there."

It was on the tip of Boone's tongue to tell her that he could take her there, maybe even bankroll the whole operation. But something held Boone back,

maybe that persistent fear that she would stop seeing him and only see his money.

He also had a feeling that Sofia wanted to do this
on her own and might not take too kindly to him
taking control. She reminded him in some ways of
his mother, who'd been a successful businesswoman
until she met his father. Even now, Deborah Dalton
ran their home like a Fortune 500 company. Pretty
much as she'd done when they were kids. Back then
there had been schedules, chores and assignments
for each brother.

She still cooked, setting elaborate menus for family dinners and those with his father's new business
associates. The heart attack hadn't slowed her down
much.

"You think you'll give Alexis some competition
someday?" Boone winked.

"Maybe. One thought is to open a wedding shop
and start there. That's how Vera Wang got her start.
After she'd worked in the business for a while, her
father gave her the money to get started."

Feeling in unfamiliar territory again, Boone
cocked his head quizzically. "I'm guessing this Vera
is a great designer."

"Um, yeah, you could say that." Sofia chuckled.
"Anyway, I'm making contacts through the boutique
and Alexis. I know she's a little pushy, but hey, that's
probably how she got to where she is. She knows a

lot of people in the business. Soon, I'm going to ask her to look at my portfolio."

"Why haven't you asked her yet?"

"I'm just waiting for the right time."

After dinner, Boone walked Sofia back to her car. She clicked it open, then turned to him.

"Do you want to come over for a little while?"

"Sure. Just follow you home?"

She nodded, reached up to kiss him and ran her fingers through his hair.

Boone followed her home in his truck, surprised when they headed to the commercial area of Bronco Valley, passing the fire station. Then she pulled into the post office parking lot, and he thought there had to be some mistake. But she parked not far from two postal trucks, got out of the car and waved at him to park right next to her. He followed her to a side alley and steps leading to a second floor. There was a balcony landing that overlooked the alley.

"This used to be my sister's place, and when she moved in with Jordan, I took over the lease. Before that I was living with my parents after college, and it was time to get back out on my own. As you might imagine, it's in the right price range for a single working woman."

She unlocked the door, then flipped on the light switch. "It's not much, but it's home."

In Whitehorn, he'd lived in a similar apartment. It hadn't been quite this small. This place was the size of his mother's new walk-in closet. Though the studio apartment wasn't much, as she'd said, the small space was clean and tidy. One room, a tiny kitchen off to the side, a small bed in a corner and a love seat. She'd made the most out of the small space, the warm colors lending it a homey, comfortable feel.

And then…her view. A side alley parking lot. Every morning he woke up to a view that most people would kill for. Big open sky, mountain ridges, the occasional deer or sheep running wild. He could hike for a day and still not cover all their property.

Chapter Six

"I just wanted to show you that I'm like you—hardworking but without much to show for it." Sofia swept her arm around the room.

He swallowed hard, guilt flickering through him. "It won't always be like this. I mean, especially once you become a world-famous fashion designer."

"Of course." She winked. "Want something to drink?"

"Thanks," he said, settling on the cushy love seat.

She handed him a cold beer, and they clicked bottles together. "To the best things in life—family and friends."

"And domestic beer," he said, to lighten the mood.

This charade of his would be over soon. If he didn't come clean, there was a chance someone else would and he couldn't have that happen. Boone would tell her before the wedding on Saturday. Wearing the clothes she'd picked out for him, he'd explain everything and she'd understand. She must know that some people with money were afraid to be liked for all the wrong reasons.

But in this moment, he had a chance to get to know everything about her with all barriers down. Without complications ensuing from knowledge about his family and how they'd come into their money.

"Tell me about your family."

"My parents emigrated from Mexico thirty years ago. They've always worked hard for everything they had, and now so do their children. We were raised with the hope that we'd do better than they did."

"Hard work never killed anyone last time I checked."

And sometimes Boone thought he'd been happier without all this money complicating his life.

"What about your parents?"

She plopped down beside him, and the love part of the seat took on its real meaning. They sat hip to hip.

"My dad had his hand in a lot of businesses for many years. Mostly a lot of fails. My mother was actually a very successful businesswoman climbing the corporate ladder."

"I love that!" Sofia tucked her legs under. "You know, my mom is the manager of the hair salon where she works. They do a good business. I always wonder, if not for all of us children, maybe by now she could have had her own salon."

"I'm sure she didn't see you kids as a hardship."

She shook her head. "We're all her little blessings, as she says."

Boone sat his beer bottle down and threaded their hands together. "What time should I pick you up for the wedding?"

"Actually, I hope you don't mind, but could you meet me there? I offered to ride with Camilla and Jordan. They have to go early."

"Sure. I'll just meet you there." He tugged her close and kissed her.

She wrapped her arm low around his waist and deepened the kiss till they were both breathless. When he broke the kiss, he framed her face with his hands.

Tell her now. The thought echoed in his head, but he silenced it. No, on Saturday he'd drive up in his Land Rover and explain everything to her. They'd have a good laugh about it, and he'd return all the clothes so they could be donated to a shelter or something. After that, he was going to start spoiling her: fancy dinners, trips, flowers, candy, jewelry. New York City. Whatever she wanted.

Sofia was the real deal.

"I better go, because that bed of yours is pretty close. If I stay much longer, you'll be in it."

Sofia chuckled. "I know I should laugh and call you optimistic."

He stood, wishing he could stay but knowing he should go. He didn't want to rush them. They had a connection and he felt like he'd known her for years.

Besides, they couldn't go any deeper with this lie

between them. She didn't know everything about him yet. Whatever negative rumors she'd heard about the Daltons she would soon associate with him. At least he'd had the chance to show her first who he really was.

He'd tell her everything tomorrow, and if he was lucky, she'd want to see him again.

She walked him to the door, holding his hand.

He kissed her again at the door, a kiss so passionate and deep that he reconsidered leaving. Maybe he should explain everything right now. "Maybe I should…"

But she smiled and with one finger against his chest, gently pushed him back. "You better go. I'll see you Saturday."

"At least it's not snowing," Sofia said on the day of the wedding.

But even without snow, the Montana autumn was biting cold. Heat lamps had been set inside the barn at strategic places, because no matter how beautiful, nothing much could be done about a drafty barn.

The barn at Happy Hearts Animal Sanctuary, which usually housed the educational center, had been transformed. The doorway was draped with soft and billowy white curtains held back by a sash. Beautiful wildflowers were set atop repurposed wine barrels on either side of the entrance. Inside, white fairy lights were strung from the rafters from one end to the other.

"Isn't it all so beautiful?" Camilla said as they carried in the wedding favors.

"Shabby chic," Sofia said. "Very classy and rustic."

"Cornelius must be having a fit," Camilla said. "Did you hear about the menu?"

"Since you've talked of little else for months, I have." With the bride being a vegetarian, despite being the daughter of one of the area's largest beef ranchers, the menu was meatless.

"We have some fish, but everything else is plant-based and absolutely delicious if I do say so myself. Our chef can create anything and make it taste good. The man is a genius."

Sofia felt all the color drain out of her face, because spotted ambling in the barn loose...was that... "Is that a pig?"

"That's Tiny Tim. He's practically the mascot around here. Did you know potbellied pigs are pretty smart? They've *trained* him to walk down the aisle and carry the rings."

"Are you kidding me right now?"

"Nope. And their dog Barkley is the ring bearer." Camilla smiled. "This wedding is all Daphne and Evan. Their love story."

"And it involves a pig." Sofia still had a hard time getting her mind around that. "Aren't they dirty?"

"Don't worry, he's pretty much a house pet. He's been bathed, and no mud will get on that gorgeous dress of yours." Camilla snorted.

"Hey, it's a Valentino. And is it wrong to want to look good at one of the weddings of the year?"

"Not wrong at all."

Together, they walked toward the section of the barn divided by another set of draped curtains and white lights. Round cloth-covered tables were gathered in groups. The food would be served buffet-style and kept warm under food lights. Hired servers from the Library were already bringing out some of the hors d'oeuvres.

And there in the middle of it stood Brittany Brandt Dubois, directing the action. An event planner, she used to work for Bronco Heights Elite Parties, but she'd recently gone into business for herself.

Sofia followed Camilla as they walked up to greet her.

"It all looks so beautiful, Brittany," Camilla said.

Brittany smiled and nodded. "Don't worry. There are more water goblets in the van."

Camilla and Sofia exchanged a look. Either Brittany was speaking into her headset to someone else or the stress of her new company's first large-scale event was really getting to her.

"I'm sorry," Brittany said, gesturing to the headset. "I so badly want it all to be perfect for Daphne and Evan."

"It already is as perfect as it can be." Camilla put a hand on Brittany's arm. "You've outdone yourself."

"I totally agree," Sofia said. "And I love your dress."

Brittany twirled. "You should. You fitted me for it last month."

"I thought that looked familiar," Sofia joked, because she never forgot a fitting.

"Excuse me, ladies." Brittany tapped her headset. "I have to get back to it. I'll see you afterward."

She walked away, muttering into the headset.

"Is Boone your plus-one today?" Camilla asked, headed toward the buffet table.

"I asked him to meet me here." Sofia wrapped her arms around her waist. "I really like him. He's so… down-to-earth. Real."

"I can't wait to meet him."

From behind her, Jordan strode up to Camilla and wrapped his arms around her. "Hey, gorgeous."

It was as if no one else was in the room.

"Hello to you, too, Jordan," Sofia scoffed.

"Oh, hey, Sofia. Didn't see you there. You look nice."

"She has a date," Camilla said. "Someone new. Boone, right? I just realized you never told me his last name."

"Dalton. It's Boone Dalton."

Camilla blinked. "Really?"

Sofia shook her head, ready to explain he wasn't one of the wealthy Daltons.

Jordan crinkled his brow. "Any relation to Mor—"

"Jordan." Jessica Taylor, Jordan's stepmother, walked up, interrupting. "I could use your assistance."

Sofia knew that must mean Cornelius was already complaining about something. Unless he'd refused to attend, something he'd threatened poor Daphne with repeatedly. Sofia had heard from Camilla that Jordan would be the one giving Daphne away. Not Cornelius.

"Excuse me," Jordan said, giving Camilla a quick kiss and following his stepmother out of the barn.

People were beginning to arrive, sitting in the rented white folding chairs whose backs were draped with a panel of burlap, a handful of baby's breath tucked inside the wrap.

Sofia had to hand it to Daphne. For a wedding in a barn, this was classy. Except for the pig, she thought as she chuckled. She scanned the space to take it all in again and saw Boone walking alone in the distance. Her breath hitched. He was wearing the wool suit he'd won, and a gray button-down. His only concession to his normal cowboy look seemed to be his matching Stetson. Stetsons were expensive, and she wondered if he'd purchased it just for today.

She met him just outside the barn. "Hi."

He reached for her hand, his brow furrowed. "I need to talk to you when you have a minute. It's important."

"Sure. Of course." Sofia pulled him off to the side because it sounded so serious. He looked worried. "Is something wrong?"

"Lord, you look good," he said, gently touching her hair.

"Thank you, sir. And so do you." She tweaked the brim of his hat. "Is this new?"

"Actually, no. That's kind of what I want to tell you. I'm—"

"Sofia." Camilla came up behind her, a frantic look in her eyes. "We need your help. A wardrobe malfunction."

"Sorry, Boone. I'll be right back." She looked around for someone she could introduce him to but saw no one he might be comfortable with, so she squeezed his arm. "Will you be okay?"

"Go. I'll be fine."

"What's wrong?" Sofia followed Camilla at a good clip, toward the building that housed the Happy Hearts office.

"I'm afraid it's Agatha."

Sofia didn't know an Agatha, but there were many of Evan's relatives that she'd never met.

"Why? She hates the dress? What did Agatha say?"

"She didn't *say* anything," Camilla said, swinging the door open. "It's more like what she ate."

Sofia gasped when she saw an old goat roaming freely around the office. "What the—"

Daphne fought back tears. "Somehow Agatha

wandered into the office and chewed the hem of my dress."

Her *vintage* dress, a billowy off-white with accents of rose and detailed sequins throughout. It was long-sleeved with a plunging neckline, fitted at the waist. Instead of a veil, Daphne wore a crushed velvet hat. She looked like a 1950s glamour girl.

Sofia went hand to heart. "Your dress? She… Agatha eats *satin*?"

"Goats will eat almost anything," Camilla muttered.

"Can you fix it?" Daphne held up the frayed hem on one side of the dress.

Sofia walked up to Daphne and put a reassuring hand on each shoulder. "I can. Just watch me work."

"If anyone can fix this, it's my sister," Camilla said.

"I'll just need to go to my car and get my emergency sewing kit."

Daphne quirked a brow, and Camilla shrugged. "Yes, that's right, she carries that with her instead of a first aid kit."

Sofia caught the comment and turned back to the women. "Fine, go ahead and make fun. But at least no one can have a wardrobe malfunction around me."

In a matter of minutes, Sofia had arranged the frayed material in a style befitting the nuance of the dress. She hiked it slightly up on one side, quickly sewed part of the frayed hemline to the bodice. It got the job done, and showcased a little leg, which Sofia didn't think Evan would mind.

When she was done, Sofia hurriedly joined Boone near the back of the barn, just before the music started up. He squeezed her hand and smiled. "This is my kind of place," he said.

He'd probably seen all the horses outside in the pastures. They were allowed to roam freely as all the farm animals were. Daphne had a good heart. And considering that a potbellied pig walked down the aisle followed by a "ring bearer dog," the only minor disaster of the day had been thanks to Agatha.

The ring bearer, a yellow Lab, made sense to Sofia. And it was such a cute idea to involve Barkley in the wedding. Apparently, his mother had been dropped off at Happy Hearts days before giving birth. All the puppies were adopted out, but a sad Barkley was returned because the owner's child turned out to be allergic. Daphne said he'd sniffed around, searching for his siblings, whimpering so much it broke her heart, so she took him into the house for the night. That night wound up being the first of many.

As the two recited vows to each other, they glowed with love and warmth. Sofia could almost feel it in the air, surrounding them, infusing and wrapping around Evan and Daphne like a cloak. At one point, Evan teared up and Sofia had to bite her lower lip to keep from crying, too. Just the way they looked at each other moved her close to tears. Even with all these guests, their vows had an air of intimacy about them.

Someday she wanted this, too. She wanted to love someone deeply and be loved in return.

After the ceremony, they were all led into the section of the barn for the food.

"I'll get us a table," Boone said.

Sofia pulled up short when she caught sight of Winona Cobbs walking toward her, looking like a showstopper in her red dress.

"Winona, you look amazing, as completely expected."

The older woman thanked her, then gestured to their surroundings. "It's beautiful, isn't it?" She gazed around the barn at all the little touches that had made this a perfect venue for Daphne and her great-grandson's special day. "But don't be dazzled by all this glitter. That's not what *really* counts."

"I know. None of that stuff matters much to me," Sofia said. "I'm here with Boone Dalton, and he's a local ranch hand."

Winona quirked a brow, and she looked a little confused, poor lady. Thankfully, her daughter Daisy walked up just then and led her to their table.

Soon it would be time for dinner and her sister's amazing food. Only the Library could make meatless dishes that Sofia would happily eat. For a while, Sofia couldn't find Boone among the throngs of Taylors, Cruises and Abernathys. She saw Brittany's

husband, Daniel, and their little girl, Hailey, heading toward Brittany. Sofia waved to Brandon Taylor
and Cassidy Ware, sitting at a table with newlyweds
Melanie and Gabe Abernathy.

But no Boone in sight. He was no longer in the
same direction that he'd headed to get them a table.
While looking for him, Sofia ran into Erica Abernathy Dalton and her husband, Morgan.

"I see my brother is here," Morgan told her after
they'd exchanged greetings.

"Oh, he is? Tell him I said hi."

Morgan gave her a weird look. "Um, he's your
date?"

Chapter Seven

Sofia couldn't believe this. Boone was one of *those* Daltons? The Daltons who owned Dalton's Grange in Bronco Heights? It was rumored to be nearly as big as the Taylor Ranch. This didn't make any sense. Why would Boone have misled her? He'd lied to her! Had her feeling *sorry* for him.

What kind of game had he played with her heart? Oh, she was going to kill him!

"Excuse me, please."

Sofia left Morgan and Erica and found Boone, deep in a heated conversation with, of all people, Cornelius Taylor.

"Of course *you* don't find any objection to this disaster," Cornelius was saying to Boone, "but my daughter is a *Taylor*, and she didn't have to get married in a *barn*."

"Now, sweetheart," Jessica Taylor said as she laid a hand on her husband's arm. "Let's not make a scene. Please. This is what Daphne wanted."

"Did you see the food? It's an outrage! Tofu, fish and vegetables everywhere I look. Bean curd, for the love of Pete!"

"The doctor told my mother that a plant-based diet is good for her heart," Boone said, his voice laced with contempt.

Nice that he was defending Daphne, when he barely knew her, but then maybe he'd argue with anything Cornelius said. Like his sons, Jordan and Brandon, Boone hadn't learned that sometimes it was best to simply walk away from the old coot rather than pick a fight over everything.

"Think what you want to, kid," Cornelius said. "With an attitude like that, I can see for certain that your family will *never* be successful cattle ranchers. Take it from me, you have a lot to learn."

"Don't tell me what I—"

"Boone," Sofia interrupted, gripping his arm. "I was looking for you. Did you find us a table?"

He turned to her, his jaw sharp enough to cut granite. "I did, but maybe we should reconsider."

Sofia realized he'd chosen the same table where Cornelius and Jessica were about to sit.

"This is fine." She took a seat and reached for his hand to pull him down to the chair next to hers.

She'd deal with *him* later. Right now, she didn't want to create a scene in front of Cornelius, Camilla's father-in-law. But when she got Boone alone, she was going to rip into him. No holds barred.

"I'll get our plates, darling," Jessica said, rubbing her husband's back.

"Don't bother. I don't eat rabbit food," Cornelius said, shaking his head and scowling.

Dinner was tense, and not just because of the seating arrangement. Sofia picked at the meal, even though it was delicious. She had zero appetite. Boone kept trying to take her hand and she kept pretending she needed it for the important business of eating. There were toasts to the couple, a speech by Jordan, then Brandon and then one by Camilla. Evan stood and thanked everyone for coming, then praised his new bride with such sweetness and heart that Sofia bit back tears.

Brittany announced everyone could now move back to the side of the barn where the ceremony had been held. All the folding chairs had been removed to create a large space for dancing. But Sofia couldn't stay to dance. Dancing made her feel joy, and right now she was too upset. She needed to find out why Boone had lied to her. Now.

She tugged Boone out of the barn toward an open area where horses grazed in the distance. Lambs, goats and chickens roamed freely. A cow lowed softly.

"Do you have something you want to tell me?" Sofia faced Boone. "I ran into your brother Morgan before dinner."

"I tried to tell you earlier, but—"

She held up her palm. "Save it. You lied to me. You're filthy rich!"

He pinched the bridge of his nose. "Listen. I didn't lie to you, it's just that I—"

"You let me believe something that isn't true at all. That's the same thing. I don't understand! I made a fool out of myself, bringing you to my tiny apartment so you wouldn't feel so bad about your own circumstances. Worried about you spending your hard-earned money buying me dinners. You drove a broken-down truck just to mess with me, didn't you?"

"Hey, that *is* my truck." He wouldn't meet her eyes. "One of them."

"Are you even a horse wrangler?"

"Yes! I work on my family's ranch and train other horses, too. I didn't lie to you about anything else, Sofia. Just my money. The rest is all true. We Daltons might be wealthy, but we're *not* accepted by the Taylors and the Abernathys of Bronco Heights. People like Cornelius."

"Cornelius doesn't like anyone, so get in line!"

"You don't understand. It isn't *just* Cornelius. We haven't been allowed to join The Association. We're treated like dirt in Bronco because we're new money."

"First-world problems, Boone! What does that even mean? Old money and new money? All money is green to me."

"It *means* that my father gambled and got lucky in Las Vegas. That's the only reason we're filthy rich.

Pure luck. It means we're a little rough for some people's tastes. We curse and we don't walk away from a fistfight. And we don't have a legacy of wealth, passed down from one generation to another. Not like the Abernathys and Taylors. Because of that, all the big ranching families here think we have no idea what we're doing. They're wrong about that, and someday we'll show them how wrong. Maybe we're a little too raw for the corporate boardroom, but I'm a cowboy. That's why I dress the way I do. It's who I am."

Her heart raced, her breaths coming short and shallow. Sofia really wanted to get out of here. She had to burn off her anger somewhere safe. She wanted to hit something. Hard. He'd lied to her. What did that say about what he thought of her?

She turned to go. "I'm going home."

"Didn't you come with your sister?"

Damn, yes, she had, with every intention of leaving here with Boone. Now she needed to get away from him so she could calm down and not smack his handsome face like she wanted to. Filthy rich! He was *rich*! The man that she'd been so attracted to, that she'd wanted to get to know on a much deeper level. How dare he be rich!

"I'll get a ride with someone." She crossed her arms, giving Boone her back.

"Let me take you home. Please." He stepped into her space, crowding her even now.

"No. I can't even look at you right now I'm so mad."

Sofia glanced toward the barn where the festivities were going on. The music, a ballad by Tim McGraw and Faith Hill, drifted outside. Daphne and Evan were dancing in the center, their foreheads pressed together. Slowly, everyone else joined in. Camilla and Jordan, Brandon and Cassidy, Morgan and Erica, Cornelius and Jessica. Clearly, there was no one to take her home unless she wanted to ruin someone else's night, too.

"Okay, fine. Just take me home. But don't expect me to talk to you!"

Boone walked to his Land Rover with an impending sense of doom. He had hoped to tell Sofia the truth before someone else did. If only he hadn't been sidetracked into that ridiculous argument with Cornelius where he'd likely wasted valuable time. But as an equine expert, he related far more to Happy Hearts than he did to any cattle ranch, including his own. He appreciated horses in pastures, grazing happily and free. And yet he was a part of both worlds. The horses on their cattle ranch had to work. But someday, he wanted them to retire like these horses at the animal sanctuary.

"*Really*?" she said, as he clicked his key fob to unlock his truck. "Um, nice ride."

He quietly opened the door, then offered his hand to help her step up. She, of course, refused it. Great. Just super.

The drive from Happy Hearts to Sofia's apartment would take them a while. He would use this opportunity to talk, even if she didn't want to. She'd said her piece; now it was his turn.

They drove in uncomfortable silence for several minutes until he finally broke it. "I'm sorry. I just wanted you to get to know me first."

"And to make sure I'm not some gold digger after your money, you mean?" She crossed her arms and shifted her entire body to face the passenger-side door.

Ouch. Well, okay, at least she was talking to him. "No."

"I've dated rich guys before. Not one of them felt they had to lie to me about it."

"Are you seriously mad that I'm not some poor cowboy down on his luck? Is it because you like a charity case, and now you're pissed that I don't need your pity?" His palms were sweaty now, and a jolt of adrenaline coursed through his body.

"Hey, I like helping people. Is there anything wrong with that?"

"That's fine as long as you're not going to judge someone who doesn't *need* your help. Whether you realize it or not, money complicates everything. And I'm guessing that you know, since Camilla is your sister. I wanted you to get to know me first. Doesn't that make any sense to you?" He hoped she heard the pleading tone in his voice.

"I feel so stupid. I should have known." She held a palm to her forehead and for the first time he heard hurt in her voice instead of anger. "You talked about your family and four brothers. Your last name. I know that Morgan has four brothers. I've obviously heard about *the* Daltons."

"You're not stupid. It makes sense that you didn't put it together." He gripped the steering wheel so tight his knuckles were white.

"You should have told me."

"And when would I have done that?" This reaction of hers, and her extreme anger, was a little unjustified in his opinion. "When I walked into the store and met you? Hey there, I'm Boone Dalton, and I'm filthy rich. Want to go out with me?"

She turned to face him, her face flushed and pink. "You could have said something the night I invited you to my apartment. We were kissing, and getting hot, and…you just should have!"

"Why do you think I walked away that night? Maybe that would have been the right time to tell you, and I almost did. I'm sorry I didn't, but damn, Sofia. You liked me enough when you thought I didn't have *anything*. Are you now going to shut me down because I have money? How's that fair?"

"Of *course* not. Whether you have money or you don't, that doesn't mean squat to me." She pointed her finger.

He pulled into the post office parking lot, and

he'd barely stopped the truck when Sofia practically jumped out.

"Sofia!" She could have hurt herself. "What are you doing?"

"Getting away from you!" She stomped up the steps to her apartment.

"Wait." He climbed out the driver's side and followed behind, sprinting to catch up. "We need to talk."

"You talk." She unlocked the front door and left it open, so he strode inside.

She was angry, all right, and he half wondered if he'd soon start ducking from flying objects. But she was worth it, even if he got knocked out cold. Maybe he'd wake up on the floor, Sofia looming over him, remorseful. Hey, a guy could dream.

"You could have hurt yourself, jumping out of my truck like that."

"I'm fine!"

She peeled off her coat, but took her time hanging it up carefully. So she wasn't pissed enough to throw it down. Or maybe she was just cautious with the expensive coat she could barely afford. For the first time, he saw this ruse from her side. It might look like he *expected* her to be after his money, but that wasn't the case at all. He had to find a way to convince her.

He pulled off his hat and ran a hand through his hair, a sense of desperation building. He might lose her if he couldn't find a way to fix this. She might be angry for a short time and get over it. But a woman like Sofia, strong and independent as she was, could just move on and leave him in her rearview mirror. He'd made a mistake and wanted to fix this, more so than he'd wanted anything in his life.

"Sofia, come here." He walked behind her, careful not to scare her off with any hint of aggression. "Please."

"What?" She turned on him, her brown eyes flashing in anger.

He reached for her elbows and gently tugged her close. "You have to understand. For me it isn't about the money. It's about my family. Okay, so I'm protective about them. Sometimes I do feel like we don't belong here, and you're the first person who made me feel welcome. Like this is where I should be after all."

In her eyes, he saw a hint of warmth replace some of the anger, and more to the point, she didn't shove him away.

"Okay?" He brought her full into his arms then and palmed the back of her head. "Forgive me for being an idiot."

"Boone..."

"I know we have something special, something rare, and I can't lose you over this."

She lowered her eyes to his lips even as her hands fisted his shirt. "I'm still mad at you. You shouldn't have lied to me. I just—"

His mouth came crashing down on hers, a very efficient way of ending this argument. But he was pleasantly surprised when the same fiery passion that had fueled her anger tonight was now channeled into kissing him back. It felt like she was giving him everything, every deep and sultry part of herself, and things quickly got hot and wild. He wove one hand through her long, thick hair and lowered the other to her behind.

In a move reminiscent of the way they'd spent every night since they met, but in reverse, she began removing his clothes. First the jacket, which she slipped off his shoulders in the middle of ravishing his mouth with her wicked tongue. Next she pulled the shirt out of his pants. When her fingers glided up and down his back, he thought he'd lose his mind with lust. Instead of losing his mind, he lost the tie, which had been choking him all night. Then she went after the button of his slacks. His pants were something she'd stayed away from altogether while styling him, acting a little shy. There was no shyness in her now.

Okay, this was happening. In the back of his mind, he thought maybe they should slow down, but surely, he couldn't be the one expected to suggest that! She was sexy, her lips soft and warm. While she was busy undressing him, he slid the zipper down her dress, a skintight blue thing that had probably been designed to torture men. It slid off her into a pool at her feet and he nearly swallowed his tongue when he saw her underwear.

She wore a plunging black bra and a matching thong that barely covered her. He took a moment to drink that in, the milky softness of her curves. Her long and luscious legs.

"You're beautiful," he managed to say.

"Aw, thank you." She smiled, then took his hand and led him toward the bed.

Boone had to admit it. This was hands down the best wedding he'd ever been to.

Sofia stopped thinking the minute Boone kissed her with such passion and authority that heat curled through her, leaving her damp. When she'd pulled his shirt out to feel the muscles she'd been lusting for, her knees went absolutely liquid. His touch traveled from her butt down her thighs where a quivering heat pulsed and ached. Under his shirt, she found those muscles were every bit the sinewy strength she'd expected. He was all hard angles and planes, and so utterly…male. So perfect.

He touched her with such intention that his hands branded her. Everything else faded to the background, and she made a decision totally out of character. She stopped thinking whether or not she'd known him long enough. She simply wanted him. Here and now. And everything else, every single doubt, flew right out of her head.

She let her Valentino gown fall to the floor, also out of character, but she carefully stepped around it when she led Boone to her bed. He gave her the slow, wicked, dimpled smile she found so irresistible and sat beside her. She'd brought him to her bed, but after that Boone took over. He kissed her shoulder, the hard bristle on his jaw rough against her sensitive skin. He eased the strap of her bra low and took her nipple into his mouth. She moaned as his warm mouth and tongue did delicious things to her self-control.

The rest of their clothes came off quickly, both of them in a frenzy. But once they were both naked, Boone slowed down. His fingers threaded in her hair; he licked the shell of her ear, then teased her earlobe with his teeth. Heat swept through her, wild and deep. She'd never wanted anyone like this. Not with this intensity. He found her mouth again and kissed her, leaving a trail of kisses down the column of her neck.

"Woman, you taste so good. I could eat you all night long."

He licked and kissed down her body, stopping at each breast to suck hard on the nipple, continuing down to her belly button, nipping at her hips. His rough and calloused hands skimmed down the outside of her thighs just before he spread them apart. She throbbed, pulsed, ached and went out of her mind. It wasn't long before her body bucked, and she chanted his name over and over like a prayer.

Sofia wasn't a virgin, but she could count her lovers on one hand, and didn't need the whole hand. She'd never had a first love, no one who burned bright and fiery, because she'd always been so focused on school. Then on her career. But an unexpected thought twisted through her mind that maybe this was what a first love should have been. What she'd missed. She felt inexplicably connected to Boone in a way she couldn't explain or understand fully.

"Come here," she said, but he was off the bed and rummaging through his wallet.

"Condom." He held it up triumphantly, and then ripped it open with his teeth.

She'd never seen anything sexier than Boone sliding the condom on his shaft, protecting her. He came back to the bed and braced himself above her, his blue eyes smoldering with heat.

"Sofia," he said on a ragged breath. "Tell me what you want."

"I want you." She ran her fingers through his thick hair. "Inside me."

"I'm not going to make you wait. And I'll never keep anything from you again." With those delicious words he plunged deep inside her.

His words were sweet, but sweeter still were his thrusts. They tugged at something deep inside her, the friction and pressure mounting, the pleasure building quickly. She wrapped her legs around his back, urging him deeper, closer, clutching at his steely buttocks. The springs of her bed squeaked, the frame rattled and the headboard smacked against the wall as Boone gave her everything he had.

Chapter Eight

Eventually Sofia came back down to earth.

Breathless, she buried her face in the crook of Boone's shoulder and neck. After a few minutes, she felt calm enough to speak.

"I'm sorry. This isn't like me."

"What's wrong?" His warm hand skimmed down to the small of her back, giving her a sweet rush of tingles.

"You should know, I don't sleep around."

"I didn't think so."

She held her breath, then let it out along with her words. "I'm not easy, Boone, but tonight I threw myself at you."

"Um, what?" He snorted.

"Seriously, I'm not usually so…aggressive. Out of control."

He pressed his forehead to hers. "You have got to be kidding me. Do you hear me complaining?"

"No, and I guess you wouldn't, but I just wanted you to know this doesn't usually happen to me."

"It doesn't usually happen to me, either." He drew

her closer into his arms, his lips against her temple, his voice deep and soft.

"I mean, my Valentino is on the *floor*." She resisted every urge in her body that told her to get up right this second and pick that piece of fashion genius off the floor. "That's how off the rails I am with you."

"What's a valentino?" He squinted.

She had to laugh. "My dress. I don't usually let that baby touch the ground."

"Why? It is holy?"

"Okay, smart-ass. It's expensive, that's all. I got an amazing deal on it. It was a sample." She threw a longing glance at the dress on the floor in a heap.

"You really want to get out of bed right now and hang it up, don't you?" He chuckled.

"Yes," she confessed. "But I won't."

"Good, because I don't think I'm ready to let go of you yet." His arms tightened around her. "It's a great dress, but what's underneath is so much better."

"Nice, cowboy. That's a great line."

He chuckled again, then kissed her shoulder. "Tell me you don't regret this. Us."

But even though maybe she'd rushed into this kind of intimacy with him, she couldn't be sorry. This felt right.

"No, I will never say that."

Boone felt comfortable, easy to be with, and in this past week she'd gotten to know the man. In a way, she was grateful to have met him before she'd known about all of the money. Having seen what Camilla went through when she dated Jordan, she might have had second thoughts. Because she'd dated rich guys before, but never seriously. She'd certainly never slept with any of them.

"Let me get this straight. You think you started this tonight, when I kissed you first?"

"You were trying to end an argument." She cocked her head and waited for him to admit it.

He smiled, a little sheepishly, as if she'd seen right through him. "You're right."

"But I'm the one who led you to my bed."

"Well, a gentleman needs an invitation." His hand gently squeezed her fingers where they were lying low on his abs.

"I ripped your clothes off." She buried her face in his neck, the shock of her boldness only now fully hitting her.

"And thank you, by the way."

She swatted his arm playfully. "You look good in those clothes! I don't know what you have against them."

"I like being comfortable, which I am right this minute." He stretched. "Except for one thing. I'm starved. Let's order a pizza."

"What's wrong?" She propped her chin on his chest. "You didn't like the pan-seared tofu steaks with coriander cream and asparagus spears?"

"I didn't see *you* eating," Boone teased, his fingers touching the soft hairs on the back of her neck.

"I couldn't. I was too mad at you. I love Camilla's food, but I'm a meat eater all the way. How many juicy burgers did you see me eat at DJ's Deluxe?"

"Yeah. You're definitely a cattle rancher's dream girl."

Those sweet words tugged at her heart, and she kissed him. Then he kissed her, a little more deeply, his tongue caressing and stroking hers. She felt his muscles tense beneath her as he grew hard again. And then Boone rolled on top of her, flashing her his wicked smile. He threaded his fingers through both of her hands, then pulled them up above her.

And they stopped talking for a long time.

The next morning, Sofia woke to the sound of the wind whipping against her flimsy windows. She and Boone were buried under layers of throws and comforters and that, not to mention their body heat, had her warm and cozy. Last night, after their second time making love, she'd hung up her Valentino, and also his clothes, while Boone ordered them a pizza.

The remnants of the pizza box were on the floor on Boone's side of the bed. Cozy though she was curled up next to Boone's very naked body, nature called. She moved, and he didn't even stir. Gathering up a blanket for cover, she tiptoed to the always-on-the-fritz thermostat. Seriously, she could see her breath, it was that cold in here. She flicked the thermostat with her finger, willing it to work.

In the bathroom, she turned on the light and startled in fright. Her hair was a wild mess of tangles, its natural frizz taking over like a weed that spread when unattended.

Great. Just great. He looks like an Adonis in his sleep. And I look like...like I just stuck my finger in an electrical socket.

She washed her face, reapplied her mascara, then reached under the vanity for the flat iron and plugged it in.

A soft knock came at the door. "Sofia? Are you okay? You've been in there a long time."

"I—I'll...be right out."

No time to fix this hair disaster. She turned off the iron and shoved it under the sink. Smoothed her hair down the best she could do and opened the door with a smile.

"Hey, there."

"Hi, beautiful." He tugged her into his arms. "It's freezing in here. You okay?"

"I'm fine, just trying to jazz up a little bit for you."

"No need. You're jazzed." Tucking her to his side, he walked them to the thermostat, holding the blanket around them both. "I think this is your problem. Seems to be stuck." He tapped it.

"I know. I need to get the landlord to fix it. Or maybe get double-paned windows installed."

"Both are great ideas, but for now let's go back to bed."

He pulled back the covers and she climbed in. He was next to her within seconds, taking her in his warm and capable arms. The fingers of one hand played with her hair, as if he didn't care that he might be stirring a bird's nest.

"My hair gets like this when it's going to either snow, sleet or rain."

"Gets like what?"

"Frizzy."

"I hadn't noticed. Well, which one is it? Snow or rain?"

She narrowed her eyes at him. "I can't actually *tell*, Boone."

He chuckled. "You didn't ask your hair? Personally, I think it might snow."

"My hair says rain. I just asked."

"It's still early, but what are you doing today? Any plans?"

She had family dinner with her parents every Sunday, but she wasn't sure that she should put Boone through that kind of interrogation this soon. Her father was hell to her dates, and he'd never met a single one he'd approved of. If he ever found out Boone had lied to her, he'd probably accuse him of high crimes and misdemeanors.

Today, she'd probably do exciting stuff like head to the laundromat, drop off some clothes at the cleaners and later work on some new sketches. The repairs she'd done to Daphne's dress had given her some new ideas.

Still, she told him, "Nothing specific. Why?"

"Might be a good time to come by the ranch. Meet some of the horses."

"You work on Sundays?" He was beginning to sound as much like a workaholic as Jordan.

"Every day is a workday on a ranch. I take time off when I need to."

"I guess I can come by if I won't be in your way."

Boone tugged her even closer, if that were possible, and shared more of his body heat with her.

She was rather curious about Dalton's Grange, having never been there. Maybe she'd get to meet the elusive Neal Dalton, who had a reputation in town as a somewhat unsavory character. When they'd first arrived in Bronco, Sofia had heard an ugly rumor that the Dalton money had come through mob connections. Another time, they were all drug dealers associated with the cartel.

But when Erica Abernathy married Morgan Dalton, she gave some legitimacy to the Daltons. No way would Erica be associated with anyone who had underworld ties. They might be a little bad, rocks instead of diamonds, but they certainly weren't criminals. In hindsight, the rumors were ridiculous. Now

that she knew Mr. Dalton had obtained his money
through a gambling windfall, she understood how
the gossip might have been started. Most people in
Bronco were conservative when it came to taking
risks like gambling, her parents included.

Outside, the wind whistled past the windows,
welcoming another crisp October day. But she cuddled closer to Boone, dug deeper under the covers
and found a way to stay warm for the rest of the
morning.

Sofia ran her errands in record time, and by early
afternoon she dressed in the outfit she'd wear to Dalton's Grange. She'd been waiting for an opportunity
to wear her new leather boots. They had a little heel,
though nothing like the four inches that were her
norm. She'd simply be watching Boone at work, so
there probably wouldn't be much walking. Anyway,
it wasn't the first time she'd built an outfit around the
shoes. She went with her thick black leggings paired
with her camel cashmere turtleneck and black faux
fur–lined vest. Because she was going to a ranch, she
decided to be casual about her hair. She straightened it, and then pulled it up into a tight and high
ponytail. At the last minute, she added a caramel silk
scarf and tied it in a perfect knot.

Boone had left her directions to Dalton's Grange,
and she found it to be a little farther out of town than
the Taylors' ranch, where she now often visited Ca-

milla. Today, the Montana sky was a gorgeous patch of blue, the mountains green and lush. The trees filled with red, yellow and golden leaves were almost showing off. A drive like this to the country was good for the soul, her mother always said.

Sofia took the turn Boone had mentioned and drove down a lone strip of road that seemed like it might be a gravel-covered driveway but went on far too long. She kept driving. At this point it seemed as if the Dalton ranch was on the other side of the moon. Good grief. Finally, she spotted a house in the distance, nestled between two hills.

Holy freaking Ferrari. They had an incredible view. On the right, she saw all the land, pastures and pens filled with cattle roaming in the distance. She found the stone-paved driveway and turned. The home was a lovely log-style cabin, very understated, and tucked close to the base of a mountain. There was a long circular driveway leading to the front, but she kept driving on the narrow lane. It led her to the barns and stables, and in the distance, the horse corral where Boone had told her he'd be.

There seemed to be a great deal of activity there, and she parked near a few trucks. She walked toward the corral, stopping when she saw a large black horse rear. The man holding the reins dropped them and made a dash for the other side of the fence. He left this mad horse in the corral with Boone.

She gasped. "Oh, no."

He was going to get injured, right here while she watched it all happen. The horse began galloping around the corral like the hounds of hell were on his heels. Boone simply stood in the center of this chaos, not moving.

"Don't worry, he knows what he's doing."

Startled, Sofia whirled around to find an older gentleman behind her. He wore a dark Stetson and looked every bit the wealthy rancher. Tall, built, imposing. His piercing blue eyes were all business, and he had an air about him that said he'd be able to take care of himself in a dark alley. No need for hired bodyguards for him. Then she noticed the large Buck knife sheathed and buckled to his belt.

"That looks dangerous," she managed, nudging her chin toward the corral.

"Not for him," the man said as he stepped beside her. "I'm Neal Dalton."

"Nice to meet you. I'm Sofia Sanchez," she said. "I'm… Boone invited me."

The horse had stopped galloping, as if out of steam. He simply trotted slowly around the corral now. Boone, for his part, walked next to him, a little closer each time.

"Horses are prey animals, so they spook easily," Neal said. "This one has a behavior issue ever since he was in an accident with his owner. Don't worry about Boone. He's handled worse. He breaks fillies and colts for us, since they're such a part of ranch work, but he does this kind of work rehabilitating traumatized horses, too."

He walked toward the corral and urged Sofia to follow him. She did, her boots kicking up the dusty ground. At the fence, Mr. Dalton stuck one boot on the rail and leaned forward.

"This is a beautiful thing to watch," he told her.

Boone had now approached the horse, facing him. The horse backed up, as if in fear. But Boone didn't retreat. Calmly, slowly, he continued to approach the horse, who backed up several more times before he finally gave up. He lowered his head and allowed Boone to step close enough to touch him.

"It's poetry in motion," Neal said.

Mesmerized, Sofia agreed. "It must take so much patience, and a complete lack of fear."

"He understands horses, and they understand him. It's like they have a unique language. My wife says that Boone loves horses more than people." Neal chuckled. "Well, maybe not *all* people, but certainly more than me."

"I'm sure that's not true."

"That's kind of you to say, but I've been a real bastard for most of my life. Boone is the middle son, and the one who always called me out on my BS. I'm sure you've heard of us. The Daltons who might not be all bad, but hell, we're bad enough."

"I don't believe in gossip. My father says that

small-minded people talk about other people. Wise people talk about ideas."

"Smart man, your father."

As they watched, Boone attached a lead to the horse and began to lead him around the corral. It looked so simple, so easy, and yet minutes ago that horse had been wild and bucking. That only meant to her that Boone made an incredibly difficult task look easy.

At that moment, he caught her gaze and gave her a quick nod and smile before he went back to giving the horse his exclusive attention.

"It was nice meeting you, Sofia," Neal Dalton said. "I'm taking my wife to dinner tonight so I better go and get spruced up for her."

"Nice to meet you."

The man tipped his hat and ambled away. A few minutes later, Sofia had finished watching in wonder as that wild horse was saddled and Boone rode him around the corral a few times. Then he hopped off and led the horse out of the corral, where he met briefly with the man who'd run out.

"Hey," Boone said, walking up to her and giving her a quick kiss. "You look beautiful."

"That's amazing. I've never seen anything like it. You've got a real gift."

He nodded, acknowledging her compliment. "Guess I speak their language. Horses get spooked easily, and I'm not as afraid of them as most people are."

"Most people have good reason to be afraid. A horse that size could really hurt someone."

"True, but they would never mean to."

"Your father reminded me that horses are prey animals."

"Did he?"

"I got to meet him just now. He's taking your mother to dinner and wanted to be sure to be presentable. That's very sweet and romantic."

It was so different from her own family. Her parents were happy and loved each other, but they rarely took time alone together. They were all about large family get-togethers and completely overinvolved in their children's lives.

"Is it their wedding anniversary?"

"No, but it's probably some other anniversary. Like their first date or something."

"That's so cute that they still do that kind of thing."

"Yeah." Boone didn't seem as impressed as he kicked a pebble on the ground. "Anything else my father tell you?"

She elbowed Boone as they walked away from the corral. "What are you worried about? He was a perfect gentleman."

"Really."

"He did use some salty language, but I'm a grown-up. It's fine."

Boone scoffed. "Bet your parents don't talk that way."

"Well, no, but you have to realize that they're very conservative."

"What would they think of a cowboy like me, I wonder." Boone draped his arm around her waist as they walked.

Her heart tugged a little because it sounded as though Boone Dalton cared very much what her parents thought of him. Sweetly endearing to a girl who loved her family.

"I think my family would like you as much as I do, once they get to know you."

"You think so? They won't judge me as being the son of a man who won his fortune gambling?"

She stopped walking, leaned in and wrapped both arms around his waist. "No, they won't. They'll make up their own minds about you. Really, Boone, they're kind people with open hearts."

He kissed the top of her head. "They would have to be, with a daughter like you."

Chapter Nine

Boone had noticed his father talking to Sofia as he worked with the troubled gelding. He'd missed the opportunity to introduce them, on his own terms, which he would have preferred.

He took Sofia's hand and continued walking down the lane that headed toward his cabin. After seeing her little apartment, he hesitated to take her inside his place for a tour, but that would happen sooner or later. While Neal was proud of his new wealth, Boone tended to feel as though he had to excuse it. Hide it. He needed to get over that, since it had nearly caused him to lose Sofia.

"That's my cabin over there," he said, pointing in the distance to a home set on a small hill. "And just east of there is Morgan and Erica's cabin which you probably can't see from here. It's close to about half a mile from mine. A little north of that and about another half a mile is Holt and Amanda's cabin."

"Gee, it's like you each have your own zip code. Every brother has his own cabin?"

"Except for Thing 1 and Thing 2. My younger

brothers still live in the main house with my parents. It's big enough that they rarely run into one another."

"I bet."

Just then a little white whirlwind came spinning around the lane, launching his body toward Boone.

"Ah, there you are, Spot."

Boone bent to pet the stray dog that had shown up on Dalton's Grange a couple of weeks ago and made himself at home. He was white with a brown spot over one eye, and no collar to indicate he had an owner. Boone had taken to bringing him into his cabin at night, thinking the nights too cold to sleep in the barn with all the other ranch dogs. Every other rancher in Bronco, hell, all of Montana would call him a soft touch for bringing a dog in the house, but ask him if he cared.

Sofia joined him, scratching behind Spot's ears. "Aw, he's so cute. Who's a good boy?"

Spot fell at her feet and rolled over, as if he'd fallen in love at first sight. "I think he likes you."

She scratched his belly. "I like him, too. Huh, buddy. How long have you had him?"

"He just showed up a couple of weeks ago. No collar, no identifying information. I nicknamed him Spot because of his eye. I asked around and no one seems to be missing a border collie mix."

"Is that what he is? He kind of looks like an Australian shepherd."

So Sofia knew her dogs. "Definitely some of that in him, too."

"He looks so familiar, but then again, a lot of small dogs look like him," Sofia said. "Border collies are good ranching dogs. The Taylors have a few."

Boone couldn't help his spine stiffening at the sound of that last name. He didn't know Brandon Taylor, but Jordan seemed like a good guy. Same with their sister Daphne. But Cornelius was such a blowhard. Those poor kids. Boone certainly knew what it was like to have a father who constantly disappointed. Neal was on a whole other level, of course, but at least Boone had to say one positive thing about his father. He was still with his first wife, the mother of his children, while Cornelius had gone through a number of spouses.

Boone and Sofia continued to walk holding hands. Though the air was cold, the sun shone brightly and with Sofia by his side, he began to feel a sense of calm he'd never felt outside of the corral.

As usual, Spot followed close behind, practically nipping at Boone's boots.

"Watch out for Spot," he warned Sofia. "He'd be a good sheepdog. He keeps wanting to herd me. I nearly tripped over him the first time he did that."

Sofia laughed. "Any sheep farmers around here?"

"Not that I know of."

They walked until they reached the end of the lane. Farther up would be his cabin, but he'd noticed

Sofia's gait becoming a little unsteady. Wearing heels couldn't be easy. She attached such importance to the way she looked. So put together all the time, except in bed. There, she was wild. He wanted to see more of that.

Boone stopped at the fence and turned her to face the pastures, filled with grazing cattle. Coming behind her, he put his arms around her waist and lowered his head to her neck. That incredible coconut and flowery scent filled him, and he wondered if she'd notice if he took a big whiff of her hair.

"It's beautiful out here," Sofia said, cocking her head to press against his.

"Peaceful. Someday I'll live in that cabin with my wife and children. It's too big for me now, but one day it probably won't be big enough."

A few quiet moments later, Sofia spoke softly. "I'm guessing you don't have anywhere to go to dinner since your parents will be out?"

"I was going to ask you to have dinner with me. Wherever you'd like. I think we're done with DJ's Deluxe for a while."

"We probably did outstay our welcome there. But I can't go to dinner with you. I have dinner with the folks every Sunday, and the rest of my family."

"Another time, then."

"Or…if it's not too soon, you could come to dinner with me."

It was not too soon for him and he couldn't deny

the pleasure that rolled through him at being asked to dinner with her family.

"Yeah? It wouldn't be an imposition?" He kissed the column of her neck, earning a breathy moan.

"Are you kidding? What's one more person? We're already a big group." She turned in his arms. "Unless you eat too much. But what the heck, I'll give you half of my ration."

He must have looked stricken, because she threw back her head in a hearty belly laugh. "Oh, my goodness, your face!"

"Okay, you had me going." He chucked her chin. "Yeah, I want to meet your folks."

Sofia decided that Boone should pick her up just before dinner and they'd drive together to her parents' house. After a wonderful afternoon meeting Mr. Dalton and Spot and being introduced to a few of Boone's horses, Sofia went home to get ready. She changed into her "dinner with the fam" style, sophisticated casual. Her family always teased her about overdressing, because they weren't exactly enforced "upon pain of death" Friday-night dinners like in the *Gilmore Girls*, one of her favorite TV shows. Sunday dinners at the Sanchez family meant that they spilled all over the house from the dining room table to the couch in the living room. During basketball season, Papi and all her brothers, huge basketball fans, ate on TV trays. Tonight might be more of the same.

But Sofia looked forward to seeing some of the clothes Boone had won tonight. It made sense that he didn't wear them to work on the ranch but surely, he'd want to make a good impression on her folks at dinner tonight.

After she changed, she phoned her mother. "Hi, Mami, I'm bringing a guest with me tonight. I hope that's okay."

"I'll set another plate. Who's coming? Alexis?"

"Alexis is my boss."

"I know, and I keep wanting to meet her."

Sofia's mother thought she should know everyone that her daughter did, as if Sofia was still in grade school. "I'm bringing Boone Dalton."

"How long have you been dating? Why haven't I met him yet?"

"Take it easy. We just started dating. I thought it might even be too soon to ask him to family dinner—"

"It's never too soon."

Sofia sighed. "I heard his father say that he was taking his wife to dinner, and so I asked Boone to join us."

Sofia figured her mother would not want a cowboy to go without a home-cooked meal.

"Mami, um, you should know that Boone is one of the Daltons from Dalton's Grange. He's the middle brother."

Sofia held her breath. Both of her parents were over-protective and they'd certainly heard a lot about the Daltons. But she knew all it would take was meeting Boone once to love him.

There was momentary silence. "He's one of *those* Daltons?"

"Hang on. We know those rumors aren't true. Morgan is a good man. I met Mr. Dalton today, and though I admit he's…a little…" Sofia was thinking of the language he'd used, the kind of salty words never uttered in her conservative Latin home. "Well…um, homegrown, a little rustic maybe. He's no one to *fear*."

"*Mija*, it takes a lot to scare me, and I'm certainly not afraid of your…um, friend? What should we call him?"

"Just call him Boone."

Sofia heard the teasing tone. Her mother probably had a happy smile on her face knowing Sofia was dating. Denise Sanchez wanted all her children married with families. Camilla was only a newlywed, but their mother had already dropped supersized hints that she hoped for grandchildren, and soon. According to Camilla, she shouldn't hold her breath.

Sofia thought of how easily Boone spoke of marriage and children this afternoon. Most of the men she'd dated would never let the *M* word cross their lips, for fear the mere thought might be contagious.

But Sofia wasn't anywhere near ready to get married, a fact that in the past had made her a favorite of guys like Brandon Taylor. She'd dated but kept it light and noncommittal. Never serious. She figured marriage was in her future someday, but so far off she couldn't even conceive of having a husband. She had a business to start and grow, and the moment she got married, her family-oriented parents would expect grandchildren. Nope. Not going to happen. She'd already been to bed with Boone, which meant he'd leaped ahead to the place meant for men she'd dated longer than six months. Not many. She'd probably have to slow things down a bit with Boone, which was why she hesitated to have her mother call him her boyfriend.

Boone arrived right on time, but when Sofia opened the door of her apartment to greet him, she couldn't believe her eyes. He was wearing a flannel shirt, jeans, his leather jacket and his usual boots. No Stetson tonight, his hair in that perfectly mussed look he obviously achieved with zero effort.

He might have noticed her full body appraisal because he tugged on the collar of his jacket. "What? Too casual? Not casual enough?"

"Why didn't you wear some of your new clothes from the boutique? You looked so handsome in them yesterday."

He scowled. "Those were wedding clothes."

She rolled her eyes and followed him to his truck, where he held the door open for her and extended his hand for a boost.

Boone buckled in and pulled out of the post office

parking lot. He reached for her hand and brushed a kiss across her knuckles.

This sent a tingle down her spine. "Are you ready for this? Don't be surprised if you're asked a lot of questions. That's just my family's way. They're over-protective of me."

"I don't blame them a bit. Okay, so your father's name is Aaron and your mother's name is Denise."

"That's right. My father works for the post of-fice, and that's how Camilla was able to rent the apartment above. Then I moved in right after she moved out."

He made a turn and then picked up with her fam-ily tree. "Felix is your oldest brother, right?"

"Yes, he's the only one that's been married. Then there's Dylan, Dante and my sister Camilla, whom you've already met. She and Jordan are newlyweds but they'll be there tonight. They rarely miss Sun-day dinners."

"Jordan seems like a nice guy."

"He really is. He doesn't get along with Corne-lius, either, so you two already have something in common."

And then there was all the wealth. They had that in common, too. No matter how it had been ac-quired. To Sofia, money was money. And she re-called with a bit of uneasiness what Camilla had been through when Jordan had chased her last year. He'd had a reputation for being a rich playboy, and

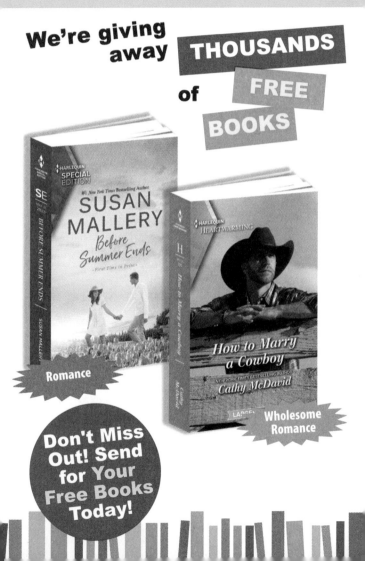

Get up to 4
FREE FABULOUS BOOKS
You Love!

To thank you for being a loyal reader we'd like to send you up to 4 FREE BOOKS, absolutely free.

Just write "YES" on the Loyal Reader Voucher and we'll send you up to 4 Free Books and Free Mystery Gifts, altogether worth over $20, as a way of saying thank you for being a loyal reader.

Try **Harlequin® Special Edition** books featuring comfort and strength in the support of loved ones and enjoying the journey no matter what life throws your way.

Try **Harlequin® Heartwarming™ Larger-Print** books featuring uplifting stories where the bonds of friendship, family and community unite.

Or **TRY BOTH!**

We are so glad you love the books as much as we do and can't wait to send you great new books.

So don't miss out, return your Loyal Reader Voucher Today!

Pam Powers

LOYAL READER
FREE BOOKS VOUCHER

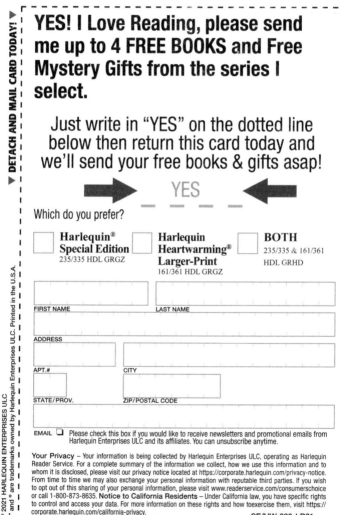

▼ DETACH AND MAIL CARD TODAY! ▼

YES! I Love Reading, please send me up to 4 FREE BOOKS and Free Mystery Gifts from the series I select.

Just write in "YES" on the dotted line below then return this card today and we'll send your free books & gifts asap!

➡ YES ⬅
‒ ‒ ‒ ‒

Which do you prefer?

☐ **Harlequin® Special Edition**
235/335 HDL GRGZ

☐ **Harlequin Heartwarming® Larger-Print**
161/361 HDL GRGZ

☐ **BOTH**
235/335 & 161/361
HDL GRHD

FIRST NAME

LAST NAME

ADDRESS

APT.#

CITY

STATE/PROV.

ZIP/POSTAL CODE

EMAIL ☐ Please check this box if you would like to receive newsletters and promotional emails from Harlequin Enterprises ULC and its affiliates. You can unsubscribe anytime.

© 2021 HARLEQUIN ENTERPRISES ULC
" and ® are trademarks owned by Harlequin Enterprises ULC. Printed in the U.S.A.

SE/HW-820-LR21

photos of him and Camilla had wound up all over social media.

Rich Playboy Jordan Taylor in Hot and Tawdry Affair with Local Waitress.

Boone and Jordan were different in that sense. Boone didn't strike her as having ever been a playboy. She didn't know any playboy who would talk about his future wife and children on a date. Even if he wasn't talking about *her* as his future Mrs., the insinuation was clear. Boone wasn't fooling around.

He'd been holding her hand since they turned onto the road leading to her parents' home, and she squeezed it. "Have you dated much since you moved to Bronco?"

"A while back, Erica introduced me to one of her friends and we went on a few dates."

"What happened?"

"Nothing. She was an old classmate of Erica's, and I think she liked that I had money. When we went to dinner, she ordered the most expensive item on the menu but didn't even eat much. On our second date, she walked me straight to the jewelry store and started pointing out bracelets and necklaces she liked. Her birthday, apparently, was coming up. In six *months*. Not surprisingly, we broke up before her birthday."

Sofia had initially been interested in Boone *because* she thought he had no money. It dawned on her that painful though it had been, Boone's lie about his money had inadvertently proven that she cared about him. And clearly, he had good reason to be guarded about his wealth.

"Gosh, I'm sorry," she said. "Money does weird things to people. Some women can get hung up on that sort of thing. You know, the flash and bling."

"Not you?"

She recalled Winona Cobbs at the wedding, reminding her not to get caught up in appearances because it wasn't what mattered. But Winona had been way off about Sofia. Glitter didn't matter to her. Fashion had nothing to do with all that. Fashion was her life. Okay, so maybe there were times when she'd been caught up in the glamour. But she'd never let it rule her.

"I dated Brandon Taylor on and off for a while, and I would have never dreamed of doing something like that. Most of the time, I tried to pay my own way, but of course he wouldn't have it. Just like you. But I don't expect any man to take care of me. That's not how I was raised. My mother always worked outside of the home."

"My mother did, too, until she got married." He paused. "How long did you date Brandon?"

"Not long. We weren't serious at all. He wound up with Cassidy. They were sort of high school sweethearts."

"How about you? Did you have a high school sweetheart?" Boone grinned. "College sweetheart?"

Sadly, she did not. She'd steered clear of anything serious in high school, worried she'd get accidentally pregnant and derail all her dreams. Even in college, there'd been no one special. Nothing would stand in the way of her dream to design high fashion.

"No one."

Boone had turned on her parents' street, and Sofia pointed out the house. "It's the second one on the right."

The single-story home was decorated for Halloween, with jack-o'-lantern pumpkins on each of the four steps leading to the front door. A toy witch on a broomstick was half on one side of a tree, half on the other, giving the appearance of having crashed.

"My father has a strange sense of humor," she told him by way of explaining the decoration.

"We'll get along just fine." Boone reached behind him and revealed a bouquet of flowers he'd brought. "For your mom."

"Oh, you get points, cowboy."

Together they walked up the short steps to the sounds of cheers, hoots and hollers inside. "I guess the Utah Jazz must be winning."

"Yeah?"

"That's their favorite basketball team. I should have warned you. Don't mention football or any other sport. Especially not tennis!"

"Thanks for all the helpful tips." He squeezed her hand. "I've got this."

Only then did Sofia realize how important it was to her that her family like Boone. She didn't ask herself why it mattered so much. It would simply make dinner smoother if her brothers didn't make any smart remarks. She hated when they embarrassed her, and they took such sheer enjoyment from it. When she'd dated a guy who happened to like tennis, they hadn't let her live *that* down for months.

Sofia didn't knock, of course, just let herself inside the family home where she'd lived not long ago. Her father was the first to glance up and make eye contact from where he sat on the sofa between her brothers Dante and Dylan. Sofia didn't miss that he sat up straighter, taking in Boone, as if he expected him to burst into flames at any moment and he'd have to jump and rescue Sofia.

"Boone, this is my father, Aaron Sanchez. And two of my brothers, Dylan and Dante."

To their credit they abandoned the TV—it was probably a commercial—and stood to shake hands with Boone.

"Nice to meet you, Mr. Sanchez. Dylan. Dante."

"Hey there, Boone." Jordan entered the room, suave and smooth as always. "I hope you like basketball."

Dylan cocked his head at Boone. "You don't like *tennis*, do you?"

He said this in the same tone of voice one might ask, "You don't like *war and famine*, do you?"

Boone chuckled. "I'm a horse wrangler, so I prefer the Kentucky Derby. Those horses have my respect. But yeah, I love basketball. It's my favorite sport involving a ball."

Sofia decided she could breathe. The Kentucky Derby comment threw her until Boone slid her a slow smile. He obviously loved to tease, too.

"Where's Mom?" Sofia asked. "Are you boys letting her and Camilla slave away in the kitchen?"

"Not me," Jordan said. "I was trying to help until Camilla threw me out."

"Whatever it is, it smells delicious," Boone said.

"Enchiladas." Her father hooked an arm around Boone's shoulder. "Why don't you sit with me, son?"

Boone handed Sofia the flowers. "Give these to your mom, yeah?"

"Okay." Sofia gave her father a look that said he better take it easy on Boone if he ever wanted her to bring a date over again.

On the way to the kitchen, she ran into Felix coming down the hall. "Hey, sis. What's new?"

"Please run interference with my date and Papi. He's going to put him through twenty questions pretty soon."

Felix was the older brother who had watched her and Camilla the most while their parents worked, and as a result Sofia felt closest to him. He understood that Sofia could take care of herself.

"Consider it interfered." Felix gave her a quick hug.

Sofia went on to the kitchen where Camilla and her mother were rolling tortillas.

"These are from Boone," she said, showing her mother the bouquet. Then she searched the cupboards for a vase.

"How kind," her mother said. "Where is your young man?"

"Papi took him as soon as we walked in the door." Sofia found a vase and filled it with water. "I asked Felix to run interference."

"Seriously," Camilla said. "No one is ever good enough for Papi's little princess."

"Is he going to give him a difficult time just because he has money?" Sofia found scissors to cut the tips of the stems and placed them in the water.

"He warmed to Jordan, didn't he?" her mother said. "At least Boone isn't a trust-fund baby. That was a tough one to get past your father. Jordan had to jump through hoops to be accepted."

"Don't you mean jump *under* hoops?" Sofia recalled the basketball game her brothers had played, Felix recruiting Jordan to his team without letting anyone know he remembered Jordan was a top-notch athlete in high school. "At least it's too cold outside today to play. Everyone here is too obsessed with basketball. Boone told them he likes the Kentucky Derby."

Both Camilla and her mother stopped what they were doing and stared.

"This sounds like an interesting young man. Brave." Her mother dropped the towel she'd used to wipe her hands. Then she walked to the doorway that separated the living room from kitchen. "*Mi amor*, you be good to that young man! He brought me flowers."

"Don't worry, I like this one!" he shouted back.

Camilla gave Sofia a smile. "Papi likes him. So, how much do *you* like Boone? More than the tennis dude? More than Brandon?"

A lot more than either of them, even put together.

"Shh," Sofia said, joining Camilla and stuffing tortillas. "I like him…a lot, okay?"

"How much is a lot? Is this serious?" Camilla pressed.

"Just because you got married doesn't mean I'm going to," Sofia told her sister. "We're *not* serious."

"Why not?" her mother asked, removing a tray from the oven and putting another one in. "When I was your age, I had two children."

"See?" Sofia said to Camilla. "Mention marriage, and children are in the next breath."

"Well, that's what tends to happen," her mother said.

Sofia and Camilla exchanged a look. Their mother was old-school Catholic.

"Do you ever imagine what might have happened if you bought your own salon before you had us kids?" Sofia asked.

"Bought? What for? I run that place, and no one can do a thing there without me."

"But it's not *yours*," Sofia said. "Camilla has her own restaurant. You could have had your own salon."

"Bah, I didn't want all the headaches." She waved a hand dismissively. "And funny thing is, the salon feels like it's mine. But your father doesn't own the post office, so why would I need the salon?"

Camilla and Sofia laughed. Sometimes it was as if their parents were joined at the hip. They had the same thoughts, the same ideas. Same likes and dislikes for music and everything else. That wasn't something Sofia would ever understand.

"I'm going to go and make sure that your brothers set the table."

When their mother left the room, Camilla shoulder-checked Sofia. "She doesn't have the same ambitions we do, and that's okay."

"I know. Maybe I just don't understand why."

"She loves styling hair, but it's not her whole life." Camilla shrugged. "Everyone's different."

"How's married life?" Sofia asked, changing the subject.

"It's wonderful." Camilla sighed. "He's so amazing. I get coffee in bed every morning, and flowers are delivered to my restaurant every day. He gave me a private office at the cabin—his idea—so that I can easily deal with any business issues that happen after hours."

Sofia was happy that her sister's life was working out. She couldn't help noticing with some pride when the horrible social media posts that once called her "that waitress" now referred to them as "Bronco Heights' new power couple. #weddingbells."

She looked up from rolling the enchiladas to make sure her mother hadn't returned. Then she faced Camilla. "Hey, did Jordan talk at all about marriage on one of your early dates?"

Camilla shook her head. "No. Remember, I didn't even want to date him at first. He asked me to give him a chance. Six dates. Pretty sure if he'd mentioned marriage anytime in there, I might not have made it through. Remember, I was just like you. I didn't want to get married and have children. But everything changes when you fall in love. Jordan and I are on the same page about children, though. No rush. We're going to wait."

"So…what do you think about a guy who mentions marriage and having a family on a fifth date?"

Camilla met her eyes. "I'd say that's a man who knows what he wants and isn't afraid to tell you."

Yeah. Sofia was afraid of that.

Chapter Ten

Boone thought the evening went well, despite the fact that he'd sat sandwiched between two men who seemed to think of basketball as some type of saintly pursuit. He hadn't been joking when he said he enjoyed basketball, even played varsity in high school. But he didn't worship at its altar. Not that he let the Sanchez men know.

Boone was relieved when dinner was ready. The enchiladas were cheesy and delicious, and people were allowed to eat instead of talk. Still, he fielded a few questions about Dalton's Grange, his parents, his brothers. He took it in stride, with the growing and unnerving feeling that this was the family he *should* have had growing up. They were down-to-earth, easy and real. If Neal Dalton had been more like Aaron Sanchez, less concerned with gambling and drinking than raising his family, maybe Boone would be closer to the man.

"My father *likes* you," Sofia said as they drove back to her apartment.

"Well, don't sound so surprised. I like him, too."

"No, see, you don't realize how rare that is. My father has never liked *anyone* I dated. Poor or rich. Although they were all perfectly nice guys, just like you. Once I even dated a pizza delivery guy."

"And I'm a simple horse wrangler."

"On a million-dollar ranch."

"Fair enough." He took her hand and squeezed it. "Are you going to hold that against me forever?"

"I wouldn't do that. I'm not holding it against you now. Watching Camilla and Jordan taught me that two people from very different backgrounds can get along fine."

"But actually, you and I had similar upbringings. Growing up, we weren't wealthy at all. Sometimes I think that makes a family closer."

"You're close to your mother. How about everyone else in the family? Are you all close?"

He considered holding back, but Sofia was so honest and open with him. "I'm close to my brothers. Morgan in particular. But as for our father, well, we've all had issues with him. I guess Morgan and Holt are getting along with him now. Not me."

"No?"

"Growing up, my father just wasn't a great role model for me. He's like Cornelius except without all the judgment about people who didn't inherit money."

"Boone, your father is *nothing* like Cornelius."

"Maybe they're just two older men I don't much

get along with. At least he's stayed with my mother, but he wasn't always good to her."

He considered telling Sofia about the cheating, but if his mother had forgiven Neal, then Boone knew this might just still be his issue. But when he thought of the way she'd been disrespected, he wanted to punch a hole in the wall.

"He seems to be very good to her now."

"He has a lot to make up for with my mother. Years."

Sofia went quiet, as if digesting that information. Boone pulled into the post office parking lot and turned the truck off. When he faced her, Sofia was studying him.

He smiled. "What?"

Instead of answering, she unbuckled her seat belt and slid as close to him as she could, given the console between them. He longed for the days of his old Tahoe with the bench seats. Her hands in his hair, she kissed him. Sweetly at first, and then the kiss grew in intensity. Heat curled through him, and he tried to pull her onto his lap.

She broke the kiss first. "I would ask you to come inside, but I think I need to slow us down."

Not what he wanted to hear, but he respected that. "Any reason why?"

"We went at it so hard and fast because there's this magnetic pull between us."

"Yeah. I feel it, too." He pressed his forehead to hers.

"I usually date a guy for six months before I even *think* about sleeping with him. You…you and I are combustible. Please, just let me have a little time to… get my bearings. You swept me off my feet, and this all happened so fast."

"What? No one has swept you off your feet before?" He rested his hand on the nape of her neck.

"Not like *this*. Never."

He chose to feel gratified about this moment, instead of believing she'd just tried to give him the kind brush-off.

"That's good. I'll give you a little time, but don't be surprised if you hear from me soon."

"I'd be disappointed if I didn't."

And with that, Boone walked Sofia to the door of her apartment, where he gave her one last kiss and then forced himself to walk away.

If she wanted a little time, he'd give it to her.

Three days later, Sofia hadn't heard a word from Boone. Not a text. No calls. Nothing. Had he simply ghosted her? She'd wanted a little time to catch her breath, but she hadn't asked him to stop calling. After texting with him every day since the day they'd met, this seemed odd. She missed his funny texts.

She got through the days working at the boutique, fitting some of the gentlemen who had come in after hearing about the new men's clothing line. Photos of Boone had been uploaded to their website and Facebook page. Needless to say, women brought their husbands in, but the ones who came in on their own wanted the "Boone special." Mostly older gentlemen, some her age, but not one of them tempting her to touch more than she had to.

Every single day, she looked for an opportunity to take Alexis aside and show her the portfolio she'd worked on for years. Each time she found a reason why she could hold off a little longer and make sure every design was perfect first.

"Thanks for suggesting Geoff Burris," Alexis told her one night at work. "A few phone calls, a little begging, and he's agreed to sign on as the face of our new men's clothing line."

"That's great."

"What about our grand-prize cowboy? How's he doing?"

Sofia shrugged. "How should I know?"

"Oh, c'mon! You think I didn't notice the sparks between you two? The way you'd head out of here hand in hand every night?"

"We went out a few times."

"And?"

"And *nothing*, Alexis."

But there *was* something. Something so powerful and intense that it scared her a little bit. He was far more serious about relationships than any other guy she'd ever dated. He seemed to know exactly what he wanted. She didn't want to get too serious with anyone. Certainly not marriage, for which Boone seemed primed. Still, the one night they'd spent together said the opposite. They were very much in sync on a physical level. And obviously, it went deeper than the physical because she really *liked* Boone. Liked how he was kind, patient, fearless with horses. He'd rescued a lost dog, obviously adored his mother and had a gentleness about him.

She glanced at her phone. Still no text messages. He listened well. She'd give him that. But this weekend was the start of the annual Harvest Festival. It would have been nice to go together. To drink hot cider and go on the hayride. Of course, she could ask him. Maybe she should.

When she got home that evening, she went straight to the thermostat, rubbing her hands together for warmth. She both conserved and saved money by leaving the heater low while at work, which meant sometimes her apartment did a good impression of an icebox.

"Brr!"

She prepared to do battle with the thermostat, surprised when it came on immediately. She heard a rattle and a hiss, but her heater worked! Hand to the grate, she felt warm air wafting out. Her landlord had finally come through.

Sofia picked up her phone to dial Al. "Thanks for fixing the thermostat."

"I wasn't able to get to it. I thought you had hired someone. Mack from Heating and Cooling came by earlier today, said it had been paid for. I was going to tell you that he always overcharges. You mean it wasn't you?"

"No, Al, it wasn't me. I was waiting for you to fix it, like you said you would."

She hung up and called her father to ask if he'd fixed it himself.

"You mean to tell me you've been freezing all this time?" Papi boomed. "I'll have words with Al!"

Sighing, she hung up with her father after talking him off the ledge.

And Sofia now had a pretty good idea of who'd hired Mack to fix her heater. She couldn't be sure, but her suspicions were strong. Her brothers didn't even know about the finicky thermostat, but if they did, they'd expect her landlord to fix it.

So, what could one say about a guy who fixed what needed to be fixed and didn't want to take the credit? Did he think her too proud to appreciate the gesture, or was this Boone's issue with his wealth? He had to know that she didn't think of him any differently now that she realized he had plenty of money.

Later that evening, she sat alone at home after cooking a frozen food entrée. Boring. Questions were rolling through her mind on fast forward. Why hadn't Boone called her yet? Finally, she could take it no more and phoned Camilla.

"Okay, fine!"

"Hello to you, too," her sister said with a laugh. "What's up?"

"I need some romantic advice, but if you tell anyone I asked, I'll deny it."

"My little social butterfly sister needs romantic advice? I mean, I'm sure you're not calling for fashion assistance. And you've never expressed an interest in learning how to cook. By the way, those cooking lessons from our master chef are still available any time you're interested, just say the word."

"Why learn to cook when my sister owns a restaurant? Yes, it's *relationship* advice. And I hate even asking, so don't make this hard for me."

"I wouldn't dream of it."

She sighed and covered her eyes, even if no one could see her humiliation. "Boone hasn't called me in three days."

"Why? Did something happen?"

"After Sunday, I told him that I'd like to slow things down a bit. It's just…hot and intense between us." Sofia began to pace the length of her apartment. Back and forth she went.

"Okay, and…?"

"Also, he wants to get married."

"To *you*?"

These phone calls to her sister really helped. Camilla asked all the right questions. She'd just figured out the root of the problem.

"Maybe not to me, but he *mentioned* it to me. And I don't want to get married!"

"I know, that's what you keep saying. I guess we'll engrave it on your tombstone. 'Here lies Sofia Sanchez, she didn't want to get married!'" Camilla snorted. "But do you want to fall in love? The two are not mutually exclusive."

"It might be nice to fall in love. I never have." She took a breath. "But Boone hasn't called or texted in three days!"

"You know, you could always call him. Maybe he's left it up to you. The ball in your court kind of thing."

"Hmm, I guess that's a good point. You're saying I should call or text him?"

"I don't see why not. This is probably not something you're used to doing, but you're the one who asked him to back off."

"I did not!"

"That's what I heard." Camilla's tone was calm, fully in her "big sister" mode.

"Well, it's not what I *meant*."

"Then I guess you better straighten that out."

This meant calling him first. Sofia never did this.

"So, you really like this guy?" Camilla said after a pause.

"He doesn't just want to fall in love. Boone is so

serious. He wants to get married and have a family. Do I have to say any more?"

"No. I figured that was the problem."

"Then what's up with that? Why can't I stop thinking about him?"

"You tell me."

"I don't know. He's just…more."

She thought of the way he spoke of his mother in a nearly reverent tone. He was obviously protective of her. And just seeing him with the sweet dog he'd rescued, and the horses…him so quiet, calm and self-possessed. It was an attractive quality, that confidence, swagger and utter ease about Boone Dalton. He behaved like a CEO of his own company but was a horse wrangler who probably never saw the inside of a boardroom. There were so many contradictions about the man. No wonder he confused her.

After hanging up with Camilla, Sofia decided she had to get out of the house or risk being the kind of woman who waited for a guy to call. Never going to happen. She hesitated. Should she text Boone and thank him for fixing the heater? How should she say it?

Thanks for fixing my thermostat. I want to see you. Come over and make my toes curl again.

Nope, that wasn't what she wanted to text. What if someone else saw it? Grabbing her coat and stepping out into the frigid evening, she decided a latte sounded good. A short drive later, she was in front of Bronco Java and Juice, watching Cassidy Ware behind the counter, filling orders with a smile. As usual, she was dressed in the green company apron, her blond hair pulled back into a ponytail. A few weeks ago, Cassidy's life had changed irrevocably. Had it been Sofia, she couldn't have coped with the life-altering accidental pregnancy. But Cassidy seemed to be handling it with her usual grace and tenacity.

Sofia didn't know Cassidy all that well, but she seemed like a nice person. Not all that long ago, Sofia had helped Brandon win Cassidy over by telling him about a beautiful red coat she'd admired in BH Couture. He'd bought it for her, and not long after the two were engaged.

It seemed that marriage was happening with so many people her age. Cassidy was known to be so serious and career-minded that Sofia hoped she'd manage both marriage, motherhood and career. It wouldn't be easy.

"Hey, Cassidy," Sofia said as she walked inside the shop.

"Hiya!" Cassidy waved hello. "Look what the cat dragged in. How've you been?"

"I should ask you that." Sofia patted Cassidy's hand. "Feeling okay?"

Cassidy certainly seemed fine. Her cheeks pink and eyes bright, her smile huge. Of course, it was too soon for her to be showing. Sofia was amazed at how excited she seemed to be. Then again, she reminded herself that for so many women, motherhood and marriage were wonderful things.

"I'm great! The morning sickness is gone, finally. Boy, not a moment too soon. I couldn't even drink my favorite juice because it made me so sick. Brandon was going out of his mind, trying anything to see if I would keep it down. But finally, I'm out of the woods."

Sofia nearly snorted. *Out of the woods?* Ha! Wait until the child was born. The denial was incredible. "Well, as long as she or he is healthy."

This was the other thing to say. Realize how much more important the baby's health was than any kind of upheaval he or she might be causing. This did seem to be true for all expectant parents, and it made sense, of course.

"Exactly! That's what Brandon says. And he thinks it's a girl." Cassidy had already started making Sofia's mocha latte, her usual.

"What do you think?"

I don't care as long as he or she is healthy.

Sofia could recite this stuff by heart now. Sure enough, Cassidy parroted the words.

"I never thought I'd see *Brandon* settle down," Sofia said, and when Cassidy's shoulders sank a little, she quickly switched gears. "But then you came along and wow. I know he loves you. I can just tell."

"Thanks. I had my doubts about him, but he's really come through."

Fortunately, with no one in the line behind her, Sofia was able to chat freely. "So…um, like, when did you know you were in love with Brandon?"

Cassidy blinked in surprise. Sofia never talked about this kind of stuff with her. They weren't actually friends, just casual acquaintances. This kind of talk was Camilla's territory. But Sofia could use a second opinion, because Camilla wasn't exactly unbiased. Cassidy at least understood what it was like to have new and strong feelings about a man you didn't even expect to like.

Sofia took out her wallet and paid. "I'm just curious. You and Brandon dated in high school, but you weren't in love back then. Something changed."

Cassidy slid over the mocha latte in its sleeve. "He's different now, but so am I. And I know what you're thinking. This baby isn't exactly what either of us planned, but I'm happier than I've ever been."

"That's good to know."

Still, Cassidy probably didn't have a plan for balancing marriage, motherhood and her business. Up to now, as far as Sofia understood, she'd been primarily a businesswoman. She even had plans to open another shop in Lewiston soon. Sofia didn't know how Cassidy would be able to give equally to both the baby and her career, not to mention Brandon. She'd have to keep him happy, too. It seemed that all of her friends who'd been married and were on their way to have children had lives that were forever changed. That's how it happened. No matter what, something had to give.

Of course, Brandon was wealthy, so they could hire nannies to help. But Cassidy, like Sofia, wasn't the type to give anything she loved less than 100 percent. How could Cassidy realistically give everything 100 percent? Clone herself?

"But…how did you *know*?"

"Why? Is this about a special guy?"

Sofia laughed, hopefully not too loudly, and waved a hand dismissively. "Are you kidding me? Don't be ridiculous. I'm asking for…a friend. Of mine. You don't know her."

"Well, you know Brandon had a reputation. The time we dated in high school we were both so young. You were the one who told me recently that you thought maybe he had a lot more going on than he let most people see. I finally saw *who* he was, beyond the rich playboy." Cassidy wiped the counter. "I fell in love with *that* guy. He's sweet and loving. He takes care of me. I know he'd do anything for me. And our baby, of course."

"That's great. But don't you ever—" Just then Sofia's phone buzzed, and she nearly dropped hot coffee all over herself trying to pull it out of her purse.

Cassidy gave her a look, her eyes wide. "Are you okay?"

"I'm just…expecting a call… Can't miss it…"

She juggled her latte, buzzing phone, Kate Spade purse. Finally, she had the presence of mind to set everything but her phone on an empty table. Had she ever in her life made such a fool out of herself over a guy? Not to mention she didn't even know if this *was* Boone. It could be someone else.

But a closer look at her phone showed a text message from him:

Have you missed all the great text?

Pure delight slid through her. Maybe he'd really been giving her the time she'd asked for and nothing more. Boone wasn't trying to rush her into anything. She'd been wrong about him and quite possibly a little paranoid. Typically, she'd overreacted. He simply liked her, maybe nearly as much as she liked him. She replied:

Life has been very boring without all the text.

Chapter Eleven

After three days, Boone was nearly jumping out of his skin to see Sofia. He'd had no more excuses to drop by the boutique, and only briefly considered going back to return all the clothes. He'd already decided to donate them to the holiday clothing drive at the Bronco Heights Community Center next month. But even if he never wore them again, they would always remind him of Sofia. The care she'd taken to select every piece of clothing for him. The way she'd touched him, her hands around his neck fixing his tie, coming so close. Her sweet scent, so warm and unique.

Man, he had it bad.

"That has to be the shortest nap in baby history," Morgan said, coming down the winding staircase, holding his baby daughter, Josie.

The moment that Josie saw Boone, her legs kicked and she reached her chubby little arms toward him.

"Hello, my best girl," Boone said, taking her from Morgan.

At almost one-year-old, she couldn't yet talk, but she certainly made a lot of sounds and pointed to what she wanted. And for a baby, she had a lot of things. Stuffed animals, dolls, a high chair, playpen, bottles, pacifiers, diapers and clothes galore. Everything seemed to be strewn over the great room of the cabin. Morgan said no matter how hard they worked, it was impossible to keep up.

Yet Boone couldn't wait for the day when he had this kind of mess take over his life. As much as he loved working with horses, lately he found it was even more enjoyable spending time with little Josie and with his nephew, Robby, his brother Holt's son. Kids were so perfect. Innocent and sweet. New. He wanted to have about six of them, give or take, now that he could afford that many.

"Let me get her a bottle," Morgan said. "Then I'll change her."

Josie pointed toward the other end of the great room, and Boone, her transportation, took her there. He set her down on the leather sectional and she reached for her stuffed bunny.

"Gah! Meep!" She buried her face in the bunny's fur.

"She really loves that thing," Morgan said. "And you know she crawls, so you don't have to carry her everywhere she points."

"Are you saying I spoil Josie?"

"Something like that."

A few moments later, Boone's phone buzzed, and he realized he'd left it at the other end of the room.

On his way to the kitchen, Morgan picked it up. "Um, do I even want to know? 'Life has been very boring without all the sex'?"

"Hey, a little privacy, please?" He caught the phone when Morgan threw it to him and read Sofia's message. "Not sex. *Text*."

"Seriously? I'm so sleep- and sex-deprived I read sex instead of text?"

His and Sofia's subtext notwithstanding, Boone would have to agree. Close enough. "What? No *sex*?"

"Not enough. Forget I said anything." Morgan returned a few minutes later with a bottle, which he handed to Boone. "So, is this text from Sofia? Or are you seeing someone new?"

"Still Sofia. Did you hear about Dale and Shep's latest prank?"

Boone assumed the position, and Josie cuddled into his arms grabbing hold of the bottle with both hands. Pretty soon she'd be drinking from a cup, and he didn't know about her parents, but Boone would miss this bonding time with her.

"You mean entering you into a contest at the boutique, so you'd get a brand-new wardrobe you'll never wear?" Morgan sat and leaned his head back, shutting his eyes.

Boone half wondered if he'd take a nap in the middle of their conversation again as he'd done last week.

"Yeah, well, we've been on a few dates. It kind of worked out for me. Things are good."

"She seemed pretty pissed at you at the wedding, if you don't mind me saying. What did you do?"

"It's what I *didn't* do. I didn't let her know that I'm one of those Daltons with money. I sort of…pretended that I didn't have any."

"Why did you do that?"

"I came to the store ready to tell her there had been a mistake, and that she should choose someone else for the grand prize. But then I *saw* her, and…"

"Kablammy?" Morgan opened his eyes and cocked his head.

He often referred to the "kablammy" and sparks he'd felt when he first laid eyes on Erica Abernathy, before she'd turned to him and revealed her swollen belly. Fast-forward a year, and now Morgan was the only father that Josie would ever know. He'd found a ready-made family.

"Boom! Bang! Kablammy!" Boone said with animation for Josie's sake, and she kicked her chubby legs in delight, giving him a sweet smile. "I wanted the real prize. Figured it couldn't hurt to spend some time together, get to know her before she found out the truth. We started going to DJ's Deluxe for dinner every night. I told her right away that my entry had been a prank. She took it well. Then she asked me to the Taylor wedding. I was going to tell her then who I was, but you beat me to it."

Morgan grimaced. "Sorry. Didn't mean to out you, but why would you keep that from her?"

"She had assumptions based on what I wear. She assumed I was poor, and I didn't exactly correct her."

"You wore your usual uniform of boots you've had for a year, jeans, leather jacket and flannel shirt?"

"Why would I replace perfectly good boots? When these wear out, I'll get a new pair."

"Well, brother, on the other hand, if she had those kinds of assumptions maybe she needs to check herself."

"What do you mean?"

A tug of uneasiness slid down his spine. Sofia wasn't one of the many women he'd met who cared that he had money. He'd proven that. Whether she realized it or not, she had a lot more going on than her beautiful exterior. If she didn't know that already, he'd make certain to teach her.

"Maybe she needs to understand there's more to a man than the clothes he wears. The appearance he projects. All the tooled leather, lariats, flashy diamond rings and ornate belt buckles. We've both experienced how appearances can deceive."

"Nah, that's not Sofia. She likes nice things. I think she likes to stand out, and she does."

"You're telling me it's her nice clothes that made you want to ask her out?" Morgan snorted.

Not even close. It hadn't even been her looks exactly. Boone had dated beautiful women who were ugly on the inside.

"It was the way she treated me when she thought I had nothing."

"Ah, well, *that's* something." Morgan took Josie from Boone and carried her into the other room. "I have to change her."

Boone glanced at his phone again. He missed Sofia, but if he wanted a life like Morgan's and Holt's—a wife, children—he had to confirm that Sofia understood what Boone believed was important. Family, traditions, connection, heritage. Boone may not have come from a legacy of ranching in Bronco, but from the moment he'd landed in this beautiful area, he'd made a decision. He and his wife would start their own legacy. At thirty-one, Boone was tired of dating and temporary relationships. He'd been ready for the real deal since he'd arrived in Bronco. He only needed to find the right woman, and he thought he'd found her the moment he first laid eyes on her.

Now he wanted to see how Sofia would do around his family, and around children. He thought of the perfect place.

"Hey, Morgan, are y'all going to the Harvest Festival this weekend?"

Sofia couldn't say yes fast enough when Boone called and asked her to meet him and his family at the Harvest Festival. She looked forward to hanging out with his family, and the festival was a favorite part of her memories growing up in Bronco. And after all, he'd hung out with her family last Sunday. Besides, Sofia knew Morgan in passing. He seemed like a super nice guy, who'd wound up falling for Erica Abernathy even though she was already pregnant when he met her. These Daltons sure weren't living up to their reputation as so-called "bad hombres."

Felix had dropped by the boutique a day ago to check in. While he liked Boone, he'd also heard that *those* Daltons weren't the nicest guys in town. He didn't care whether or not they were accepted into the Bronco cattleman's association, but just wanted to make sure Boone was treating her right.

She assured him that he was.

The Harvest Festival was held annually on land near Bronco's largest local pumpkin spot. Sponsored by some of the wealthiest ranching families, it'd been going on for as long as Sofia could remember. The local schools included one weekday field trip during October, where busloads of kids would descend on the place. There were rows upon rows of orange and yellow marigolds, and heaps of pumpkins of every size for sale. In the middle, a pyramid of pumpkins was around twenty feet tall. As a child, Sofia had loved the train ride that traveled the entire farm, going around the pumpkin patch, past stuffed scarecrows and the corn maze. The hayride on a wagon was another attraction, but there were also plenty of carnival-style games and food exhibitions.

It had rained two days ago, so the ground was still soft and muddy in places. Sofia got out of her car and stepped carefully around it all, though she'd worn her favorite snazzy rain boots today, the ones printed with pink umbrellas. At the entrance, Sofia caught sight of Boone, waiting, hands stuck in the pockets of his jacket. That leather looked comfortable, worn in all the right places, and a sudden memory hit her swiftly. She'd loved a blue-and-yellow cotton dress with a pattern of sunflowers when she'd been a child. She'd loved it, not just because it had looked so good on Camilla before she handed it down to Sofia, but because the material was soft and gentle on her skin. Comfortable. She had begun to think of Boone in the same way.

Plus, the jacket Boone wore gave him an attractive, kind of bad-boy vibe, even if he was clearly no such thing. This cowboy might dress down, but Sofia understood there was a lot more depth to Boone than she'd realized.

As she approached, a couple of teenage girls descended on him, tossing their hair and licking their lips. She understood, because as a teenager she'd gone for the bad boy too. Those guys who never wanted to settle down with just one girl made it safe to date them. Nothing ever got too serious.

The girls might have asked him for directions, because Boone pointed and spoke, until Sofia caught his eye. He smiled then, seemed to excuse himself from the girls and walked toward her. The girls stared dreamily after him, somewhat crestfallen when he walked away.

"The Boone Dalton fan club?"

When he reached her, he stopped and pulled her into his arms, giving no mind to the fact that couples walked around them on their way into the festival.

"I missed you, woman." He spoke into her hair, giving her an all-body shiver.

"I missed you, too. And thank you for hiring someone to fix my thermostat."

"Ah. You figured that out."

"It didn't take me long. That was kind, but you should have let my landlord pay for it."

"Sorry, but I couldn't stand the thought of your cute ass freezing every night I wasn't there to keep you warm." He took her hand and tugged her through the entrance, joining the throngs of residents. "Morgan and Holt are already inside. Robby is in line for the train ride. The new parents, of course, are taking photos of Josie over by the pumpkins."

They walked hand in hand past the petting zoo near the entrance sponsored by Happy Hearts, and all the tents with games. In the distance near the rows of colorful marigolds, she spotted Morgan holding Josie while Erica snapped one photo after another. The baby girl was cute, blonde and the image of her beautiful mother. She should be turning one soon, because nearly a year ago, Erica almost gave birth at the Denim & Diamonds party on the same night Camilla met Jordan.

"Hey, guys!" Morgan said, waving to Boone and Sofia. "Beautiful day, huh?"

The sun indeed had graced them today in full force, raising the temperatures to more bearable levels.

"But the forecasters said it might snow," Boone said.

"It still could," Erica said, taking the baby. "You know how it is. This good weather won't last. Boone, would you take one of all of us? Selfies are hard with a baby."

Boone let go of Sofia's hand and took a few photos of the happy family of three. Sofia didn't have to look through the lens to feel the love that radiated from this couple. And little Josie, right in the middle of all that adoration, just seemed to glow with the energy.

"We really ought to get a photo of us on the hayride," Erica teased. "Last time we were here together I was huge. That's where he first kissed me, you know?"

"It was sort of our first official date." Morgan tugged her close.

Once Boone gave the phone back and Erica checked the photos, Sofia noticed that Josie squirmed in her father's arms and began to fuss.

"She wants her favorite uncle," Morgan said, and handed Boone the baby.

Boone took her with practiced ease. "How's my favorite girl?"

Little Josie cooed, smiled and blew a raspberry.

"She's exhausting, that's how she is," Erica said, going into Morgan's arms. "She's still not sleeping through the night."

"Don't worry, someday soon she will." Morgan kissed Erica's temple.

"I have heard that she might sleep better if we had a family bed—" Erica said.

"No," Morgan said. "We tried that."

"But as you can see, my husband isn't fond of the idea." Erica rested her head on his shoulder.

A little boy came running up to them, a couple following close behind. "Uncle Boone! I went on the train ride. And there's a haunted house! Also, pumpkin pies and pumpkin ice cream!"

The kid practically levitated in excitement. Boone ruffled the boy's hair. "Robby, meet my friend Sofia."

She was then introduced to Holt, Robby's father, and his new wife Amanda.

"Are your younger brothers here?" Sofia asked. "Your parents?"

"This isn't really their thing," Boone said, handing Josie back to Erica. "Hey, Robby, want to go get some of that pumpkin ice cream?"

"Yesss!" Robby turned to Holt. "Dad? Can I?"

Holt nodded, and Robby grabbed Boone's hand. "Let's go, dude! Before he changes his mind."

"We're going to freeze, but that's half the fun." Boone took Sofia's hand and they walked to the tent selling ice cream.

Brave Robby got a cone, but Sofia decided she only wanted to share a cup with Boone. She loved ice cream, but call her crazy, come October she liked her pumpkin in a hot latte. They must have made a funny picture, all three of them dressed warmly and eating ice cream. But even when the sun came out, the temps only rose to the low fifties.

"Ew, you're sharing? What about cooties?" Robby made a face.

"Buddy, I like her cooties," Boone said, offering her a spoonful.

Sofia took some, but her teeth protested. Next, her brain froze. "That's enough for me."

"Okay, wimp." But Boone pulled her close into his arms, lowering the zipper on his leather jacket and tucking her close.

Cozy and snug, she felt desire thrum through her. His touch was both comfortable and easy but also spiked her emotions with something close to longing. Her body buzzed when she buried her face in his warm neck.

"Is Sofia your girlfriend?" Robby studied them, his tongue now orange, face a tinge of blue.

"Yeah, this is my girlfriend," Boone said. "Why? You like her?"

Sofia peeked out from Boone's neck, wondering if the little boy who appeared to be in the early stages of frostbite would approve of her.

"Are you okay, sweetie?" she asked.

He nodded his head, or was he shaking from the cold? "I'm c-cold, Uncle B-boone."

"What a shocker. C'mere, buddy." Boone set the cup down and held out his free arm to Robby. "Get warm."

Boone held his warmth like he had his own furnace. Sofia's arm curled around his waist, and he kissed the top of her head. The threesome stayed that way for several minutes until they were joined by Holt and Amanda, laughing softly.

"They're about to choose the biggest pumpkin, Robby," Amanda said.

"Gotta go, dude!" Robby, fully regenerated, jumped up. "Thanks for the ice cream!"

After they'd left, Boone stood there, still holding her close. "Want to go to the petting zoo, little girl? We passed it on the way inside."

"I'm dying to see how heavy the winning pumpkin is, but yeah. Let's go see the cute goats."

"It's sponsored by Happy Hearts." He tugged on her hand.

That meant that Daphne had not only had time to run a business, fall in love and plan a wedding, she'd also taken this on. The woman was a dynamo. Next to the petting zoo was another separate area with dogs and puppies up for adoption. Children and parents played with the dogs.

"I'm surprised that Holt was able to walk by this display without Robby begging to adopt another dog. But they have to go back out this way, so I'm not sure the luck will hold."

"Oh, hey, Boone!" One of the teenage helpers inside the fenced-off area greeted them. She was blonde and pretty, and obviously half in love with Boone.

Boone handed over some tickets to her, but she didn't accept them. "Are you kidding me? You should be allowed in free after your fat donation! Happy Hearts sure appreciates it."

This close to Boone, Sofia felt him tense beside her. "It was no big deal," he replied.

"No big deal? Our office manager practically jumped in the air and said Daphne would be so happy!"

Once they were inside the pen, Boone squeezed her hand. "It's for a good cause."

"You don't have to explain yourself to me."

But the thought that Boone would support a charitable organization like Happy Hearts wrapped around her heart like a soft blanket.

"I've always been interested in starting a horse sanctuary of my own."

He went on to tell her about wild horses, and how too many of them were taken into Mexico and Canada to be slaughtered. How in Nevada, ranchers were concerned over wild horses grazing on wheatgrass meant for Angus cattle. There were far more horses than could be reasonably supported on the public land.

"It's become a problem, but I can't believe the answer is killing those beautiful creatures."

"Now you can afford to do something about it."

"Maybe that's why I don't spend much money on myself. There's so many great animal causes." He bent to pet Tiny Tim, the official ring bearer from Daphne's wedding not long ago.

"Watch out for Agatha," Sofia warned, recognizing the goat. "She eats clothes."

"Thanks for the warning." Boone chuckled. "Was that the wardrobe malfunction at the wedding?"

"You know it." Sofia bent to pet a sheep and laughed when Agatha tried to headbutt Boone's leg. "All animals love you, Boone. Agatha is trying to get your attention. Or maybe she'd just like a taste of your shirt. Face it, you smell good."

Sofia went on to have her fun naming the goats. "That's Agatha, so this one is Betty, this is Charles, and finally, here's Debbie."

"Alphabetical order? Lame. Okay, you don't get to name our kids."

Before Sofia could fully process that staggering sentence, out of the blue, a flash of brown leaped in her direction, and before she could even turn, she went flat to the ground, tasting mud and damp grass.

Chapter Twelve

"**B**ad dog!" someone yelled. "How are you ever getting adopted if you pull stuff like this?"

"Sofia, baby, are you okay?" Boone pulled her to a standing position.

He had watched helpless as she got knocked over by the dog who'd leaped the fence. He tried but couldn't stop her forward momentum. Sofia had mud…everywhere. She spit out grass and brushed back strands of dirt-encrusted hair. How she'd been hit that hard he'd never know, but it probably hadn't helped that she'd been crouching to pet a goat. She'd sort of slid across the ground and braced a second too late. It would have been funny had it been one of his brothers.

"I think so. What h-happened?" She rubbed at her elbow.

"A sheepdog jumped the fence. Guess he thought he had a job to do."

"Sorry, miss. That never happens. He's new," the teenager said, handing Boone a wet paper towel. "Here."

Oh yeah, that ought to do it. A single paper towel.

He didn't know if he should start with her black leggings first, or the white fisherman's sweater. Formerly white, that is.

She rubbed at her disheveled hair, appearing a bit stunned. "I'm okay."

Boone wiped at her nose smudged with mud. "There."

"Well, I was overdue for a clay mask at the spa," Sofia joked.

"That's my girl."

"I want to go home now," Sofia said. "I need to change."

"I'll take you back to my place. It's closer."

"But—"

"Don't worry. You can take a shower and get all that mud out of your hair."

She looked back as he led her through the gate. "Is the dog going to be okay? They're not going to punish him, are they?"

"Don't worry, he must have been auditioning for some rancher. After work like that, he'll be adopted in a nanosecond."

"Boone, I should really go home. I have my car, and—"

"Do you want to get the interior dirty?"

"What about *your* truck? You have a nicer interior than I do."

"I drove my clunker truck today. Robby says it

feels like a roller-coaster ride." He pulled out his cell. "I'll just text Holt and Morgan that we're leaving."

"Just take me home and come back to enjoy the day with your family."

"No. I'm taking care of you. Neither one of us saw that coming, but I'm the wrangler. I should have sensed that whirlwind coming out of left field."

Chalk it up to being too engaged with Sofia, as she named petting zoo animals in alphabetical order. Hand on her back, he steered her past the crowds and led her to the asphalt parking area, where he helped her into his truck.

"Was it my imagination or were people staring?" she asked after he got in. "I must look like something from a horror movie." She smoothed more of her hair down, the red now tinged with brown.

"I didn't notice, but I for one love this new look."

She slid him a deadpan look. "Sure."

He was only partly lying. Of course, he'd noticed the stares, the frowns of concern, but he liked Sofia messy. For the first time since he'd met her, it felt as if she actually needed him, and not the other way around. Surely he couldn't be blamed for enjoying that feeling. He drove back to Dalton's Grange, this time taking the side road that led more directly to his cabin and bypassed the main house. He helped Sofia out of the truck and led her up the stone-paved lane to his wraparound porch.

He opened the door he'd left unlocked and waited

for her to walk through before he closed it behind them. Because Sofia had dated Brandon Taylor, he assumed a cabin like his wouldn't be all that impressive. Still, he tried to see it through her eyes. Boone had had it designed with a decidedly Western theme, homey and comfortable. The lower floor wrapped around in a big circle, with a more formal living room to the right that led to the large and open kitchen. To the left, the great room also wrapped around and met the other side of the kitchen. Not far from the foyer was the staircase that led to the upstairs bedrooms. He had three. Yeah, yeah. He was a single guy who didn't need that much room. But he'd built for the future he envisioned. A wife, lots of kids running around.

They were greeted by Spot, who immediately recognized Sofia, wagging his tail and yipping several times.

"I'm still having no luck finding his owner."

Sofia bent down to pet Spot, who rolled over on his back and then sighed in bliss when Sofia scratched his belly.

"This is a nice cabin," Sofia said as she stood up and looked around. "So, where's the shower?"

Nothing like cutting to the chase, he thought, but she probably felt uncomfortable. He held her hand and led her up the steps, but rather than presumptively taking her into his bedroom, led her to the guest bathroom down the hall.

"I'll be right back," he said, and went to find fresh towels. When he returned, he handed her a plush terry cloth robe. "You can wear this when you come out."

Biting on her lower lip, which might have been concealing the start of a smile, she gently pushed him out of the bathroom and shut the door. Until then he hadn't realized he'd been lingering.

Okay, then.

Naturally, he'd fantasized about this moment. Sofia here, alone in his cabin with him, where he could take care of her and spoil her. But this wasn't the way he'd imagined it. She should be here because she wanted to be, and not because some mad sheepdog had shoved her headfirst into the ground. When he'd turned her over and helped her stand, she'd been dazed.

Anyone could see that Sofia had never been the slightest bit of a tomboy. Her nails were always perfectly manicured, her makeup flawless. Every hair always perfectly in place, outfits so well coordinated that even someone as fashion-clueless as he sat up and took notice. But even so there was never any hint of superiority from her. She was down-to-earth and approachable. Kind and compassionate. He'd honestly never met a woman quite like her. Sure, he didn't understand why she was so meticulous about her looks, when clearly, she had a lot more going on. She was intelligent, strong-minded and creative.

He busied himself by starting a fire in the fireplace downstairs. Then he went in the kitchen and shoved away evidence that he was a bachelor who liked to snack on beef jerky and cold beer. Thankfully, everything was clean, and all dishes put away. But as he looked for actual food, he found nothing. He didn't cook much these days. Either he went out for dinner with his younger brothers, or Morgan and Holt invited him over. Even though his mother invited him to dinner every week, Boone mostly avoided sitting at the table with Neal. There were times when his mother brought him dinner because she couldn't stand him to go without a home-cooked meal.

She was a rancher's wife through and through, a saint of a woman who put her family first. Just like Sofia's mother.

Boone was stoking the fire when he heard soft footsteps on the staircase and turned to see Sofia, wrapped in his oversized white bathrobe. She had a towel wrapped tightly around her head and held her clothes. Fresh faced and devoid of make-up, she was still stunning. His heart hammered away in his chest.

She met him at the base of the steps. "You don't have a blow-dryer. Or any hair products."

"Sorry."

"Don't be. That hair of yours is obviously a gift from God." She smirked.

"I told you, it's called the wind." He shoved a hand through his hair and took her damp clothes.

"They just need to be hung to air-dry. I managed to spot-clean them. It wasn't as bad as it looked. I guess my face and hair took the worst of it."

"I made a fire for us." He took the clothes and hung them up to dry in the mudroom.

When he returned, she sat on the fireplace hearth, legs pulled up to her chest, staring inside at the licking and sparking flames.

She stole his breath.

Her long, bare legs peeking out from under the robe were driving him to distraction. Was Sofia completely naked under there, or had she put her bra and panties back on? He wanted to know.

And there was only one way to find out.

As Sofia sat in front of the fire, she admired the room. There was a sectional couch and a couple of recliner chairs. Everything looked either new or barely lived in. The ceilings were vaulted, giving the room an open look with tall windows that let in plenty of natural light. She wondered if he spent much time in this cabin. He hadn't been in Bronco long, so this could all be new construction. The wood smelled new and mingled with the light scent of pine drifting into the house.

An amazing view through the windows and glass sliders revealed part of the explanation for the pine smell: a forest of pine trees and a creek in the distance.

The house truly was amazing. She'd especially

enjoyed the luxurious guest bath, with its claw-foot tub and glass-encased shower big enough to fit a group. Different-sized stones adorned the walls of the bathroom, creating ledges for decorative votives. It was like something out of a Western magazine.

The whole time she'd showered, she'd kept reminding herself that this wasn't seduction time. She'd simply dry her clothes, enjoy a tour of his house and get Boone to drive her back to her car. They'd agreed to slow down since that first crazy, impulsive night together, and she for one still meant it. Mostly. When she and Boone were together again, she'd know him better. And she had to admit that today had taken a big leap in that direction.

She heard a noise and looked up to see him walk back in the room, the picture of a classic mountain man. Jeans, flannel shirt, boots, light scruffy beard.

He made this look *work*. It certainly worked for her.

She smiled as he settled behind her, pulling her back to his chest. Spot, who had followed Boone, now settled himself on a little dog bed not far from the fire. He turned several times in a circle, then lay down with a big doggy sigh.

"It must be rough," she said with a chuckle. "Living like this."

"You're right, I can't complain." He lowered his lips to the column of her neck, sending a little shiver down her spine.

"I'm really happy for you. You're lucky."

She'd guess not too many people enjoyed this kind of bounty from a father's gambling windfall. In the next breath, she felt guilty for thinking that. It might be what their detractors thought of the Daltons. That they hadn't earned their wealth through hard work or family legacy but pure luck. That somehow what they had wasn't good enough because of the way they'd acquired it.

"How are you doing? Feeling better now?" He skillfully changed the subject.

"Much. My hair is free of mud and grass. I just wish I had gel or a blow-dryer. You didn't have either in the guest bath. In your own bathroom, maybe?"

"No, sorry."

"It's just that my hair does this weird thing when it dries on its own."

"Does your hair say rain or snow today?" He couldn't hide his smile.

"Wouldn't you like to know?"

"I think you're beautiful," he whispered near the shell of her ear. "Just as you are."

Those words stilled her, and in that quiet space she felt a profound sense of peace.

He helped remove the towel from her hair and she fluffed it out, resigned to letting it dry in front of the fire. Unmanageable waves or not. Her hair was one of her biggest gifts and greatest curses. It definitely had a mind of its own.

"Do you want something to drink? I have coffee."

"Sure."

Boone was a whirlwind. A great host so far. But earlier today, he'd mentioned children, even if joking, and she'd nearly had an aneurysm. Who mentioned having *kids* with someone when they'd just started dating? Was this normal, or had she just always dated commitment-phobes like herself? She made a mental note to ask Camilla.

When he came back a few minutes later, she'd moved onto the sectional. He offered her a mug and sat close, his muscled thigh next to hers.

"Boone," she asked carefully around the rim of her mug. "Were you ever…um, married before?"

"Nope. Never married before."

"Close?" she pressed. "High school sweetheart?"

He already knew that she hadn't had a sweetheart at that age, but she'd never asked him.

"No high school sweetheart. Too busy with school, working and wrangling horses. I wish I'd made more time to date and hang out with friends."

She cleared her throat, eager to change the subject. Casual dating had always been fine with her, and all she needed. Now she wondered if she'd missed out on something pretty wonderful like falling in love.

"I noticed something today. You're really good with kids."

"Think so?"

"Little Josie lit up when she saw you, and Robby knew he could count on you for the ice cream."

"I probably spoil them too much because I get to be the fun uncle. I won't do that with my kids."

There he went with the kids talk again, although she supposed *she'd* brought it up this time. "You... want kids?"

Sofia had to ask because she wondered if she was somehow auditioning for a part she didn't want. Wife and mother.

"Sure, yes, I want kids. What about you?"

"It's a big commitment."

Wow, Sofia, truer words were never spoken, were they?

In her large and conservative Latino family, children and family came first. It would be irresponsible not to eventually want all of those things. Sofia knew she *should* want them. She couldn't help that she didn't, and occasionally guilt would thread through her like a needle looking for a place to pinch.

Boone simply studied her, as if waiting for her to say more. Because surely, there had to be more. But Sofia had honestly never thought of herself as a mother for longer than two minutes. Kids were cute, sure, but as the youngest in her family, she'd had little to no experience with babies. *Someday* she assumed she'd be a mother, but she had put little to no thought beyond that.

"And I'm only twenty-six." Did that sound defensive? She hoped not.

"Oh, yeah? I'm thirty-one."

"I didn't know that."

She didn't think he looked thirty-one, not that he was old. But they certainly might not be in the same place when it came to relationship goals with their five-year age difference. Still, when she looked at Boone, she knew without a doubt *he* was what she wanted. She wanted a man with this kind of easy confidence, who wasn't afraid to stick up for his family, to fight the world on their behalf if he had to. It reminded her a little of her own father, and how much he believed in family and honoring and respecting one another.

"So when I was a freshman in high school, you were a sophomore in college."

"Am I too old for you?" He winked, running a hand down her waist to her hip, and even through the robe she felt his hand branding her, waking her up.

"Hardly." She took one last sip of her coffee and set her mug down, then turned to give him her full attention. "I'd say you're just right for me, in so many ways."

This was the God's honest truth, even though it scared her spitless. The more she learned about Boone Dalton, horse whisperer, the more she wanted to know.

"I feel the same. But I heard what you said loud

and clear. You want to slow this thing between us down, and I respect that. Even though this might be the most romantic situation I've ever been in, I'm not going to seduce you." His blue eyes darkened, and he spoke after a long beat of silence. "Unless that's what you want."

Gulp. She wanted him so much, wanted those big, strong, calloused hands that could be so gentle. That mouth that knew how to kiss her so that she only craved more.

But before she could say anything, he took her hand in his, pulling her up, and she was certain he'd read the invitation in her eyes. But instead of leading her up the staircase to his bedroom, he tugged her close to the end table and picked up a nearby remote. Music came on, a light and breezy country song that was a favorite on her playlist. The superior stereo sound surrounded them.

"This is from my Spotify."

Well, he couldn't have planned this better if he were a psychic. It reminded her that Winona, the so-called town psychic, had picked Boone's entry. *This is the one,* she'd said. *You've been searching.* Up until this moment, Sofia hadn't thought Winona meant anything other than the contest winner. But she was beginning to wonder if this overwhelming feeling she had for Boone was what people meant by falling in love. If that were the case, then it had happened at first sight. She didn't know what to make of that. It sounded about as whimsical as being psychic.

Boone took her hand in his and spun her around the room effortlessly. Sofia was no slouch when it came to dancing, having spent many a weekend over the past few years on a dance floor. But that had been with her girlfriends, and any brave male willing to join them.

There hadn't been many of those men who could dance without stepping on her toes a time or two. But Boone was graceful as he led her around the room, and they both laughed, keeping perfectly in time with each other. When the song ended, he dipped her. His earnest face above her, those irresistible dimples flashed. Her heart tugged powerfully.

They danced to two more songs, both also on her playlist.

"You're good at dancing, too." She put her hands on her hips and gave him a sidelong look. "Is there anything you can't do?"

She expected him to say that he couldn't bake, sew or iron a shirt. Typical alpha guy stuff.

"Forgive," he said, not meeting her eyes. "I'm not good at that."

The confession was unexpected. "Not many people *are*. I think it's just a matter of time if you're willing."

"I don't know about that." He shrugged. "It's been

a few years now and I can't seem to forgive him. I've tried."

"Are you talking about your father?"

"Good guess." He led her back to the sectional.

"What did he do that was so awful? Gamble? Drink too much?"

"At different times all of that, but he also cheated on my mother."

The words sliced through her, the pain in Boone's voice nearly palpable. She could only think: *That nice man who seemed so proud of his son's horsemanship?* She couldn't imagine what it would be like to know such a thing about your own father. Your hero. Tough way for him to fall from a son's grace.

"That's awful." She squeezed his hand.

"Sorry to bum you out like this. It's something I've been thinking about lately. I need to figure out how to get past this. Forgive him. My mother wants me to."

"Be gentle with yourself. It's not an easy thing to do."

Boone ran a hand through his hair. "She gave everything up for him. Her corporate career wasn't something she could continue to do out on a ranch, and his entire life was ranching. So she pulled up stakes. Gave it all up to be with him and raise a family. Then that's how he rewards her. A slipup, my mother calls it. The woman is a saint. I don't know *how* she forgave him."

Sofia was now even more impressed with a woman

she'd yet to meet. "That kind of forgiveness…that can only come from real and unconditional love. She must love him a lot."

"Yeah, she does." He palmed her thigh. "We should all be that lucky. She tells me that if she forgave him, I can, too. And it's true that my father used to drink a lot back in those days. He gave up drinking after my mother had her heart attack, just before he bought this place."

"That says something. Drinking too much goes along with so many careless behaviors. If he's given that up, maybe he is a new man."

"Like I told you, my two older brothers have reconciled with him. Morgan, because I guess they bonded over becoming fathers. Dad helped Morgan with that transition from going immediately from falling in love with a woman to becoming a father."

"And you? Is there anything he can do? A way he can make things up to you?"

"He wants to help me get my name out as a world-class horse wrangler. Maybe start a side business. But I don't need his help."

That seemed rather shortsighted to Sofia, but she simply pressed her lips together and said nothing.

Boone kept going. "He seems to think that if he helps me then I'll easily forgive everything he's done in the past."

"I hope you find a way to forgive your father someday."

"Yeah. Me, too."

Even if she found cheaters to be one of the lowest forms of life on earth, as low as an earthworm, this sounded like a different situation. She found herself not wanting to place blame for once, but on the other hand, she was decidedly on Boone's side. It was laughable to even *think* of her father cheating on her mother, but if he did, Sofia would want to forgive him. She had learned that hanging on to grudges only hurt the person left holding them.

They sat together quietly for several minutes. It was a calm and peaceful moment, not a boring or awkward silence at all. This felt serene. Comforting. They already had the easy kind of natural lulls in conversation that Sofia had only experienced with family.

Boone seemed to absently glide his hand up and down her spine in a soothing pattern. She pressed against his shoulder and a sense of relaxation enveloped her. All she needed was a blanket and she would fall asleep in his arms within seconds.

As if he sensed that she was enjoying the cuddling a little too much, Boone palmed her neck and pulled her to face him. He wore an almost mischievous smile.

"Hey, you feel like going outside for a while? There's something I want to show you."

Chapter Thirteen

Boone waited for Sofia to change, planning what he hoped would be an afternoon of riding.

"Where are we going?' she asked, coming back down the steps to meet him.

"For a ride."

"But I—"

"You like horses?"

"Sure, I do, but it's been a while. I was much younger when I rode. My father made sure all his kids learned how to ride, but Camilla was the one who barrel-raced. She was also the junior rodeo queen one year. So was I."

He handed her a hat, and she tucked most of her long hair inside it.

"Impressive. And as long as I live in Bronco, you have an open invitation to Dalton's Grange."

Speaking of invitations, he hadn't taken the one he'd seen in her eyes earlier. Because, first, maybe he'd imagined the whole thing. She'd need to say the words to him out loud. Secondly, he also wanted to be sure that the next time they hooked up it wouldn't just be hot sex. It was going to be next-level. A deep intimacy unlike he'd ever experienced. He looked forward to that. With her, that was within reach, and he sensed it. Now he couldn't settle for anything less.

Somewhere in between the first time he'd laid eyes on her and today, when she'd laughed and danced with him, he'd made a decision. A possibly life-changing choice, but he'd rarely felt as certain of anything in his life. Sofia was it for him. Forever.

It scared him to think he'd fallen for someone a bit younger than him, someone who didn't seem ready for all he wanted from her. He'd try to be patient and wait for her to catch up to him. Just because he'd fallen in love at first sight didn't mean that it had been the same for her.

In the mudroom, he handed her another of his well-worn leather jackets. "I know it's not fancy or what you're used to. But just for today."

She shrugged into it. "It's comfortable."

"I don't care what you wear, baby, you always look gorgeous."

"I'm glad you think so, anyway." She rolled up the sleeves of the jacket.

With Spot following them, Boone led her to his private stables where he kept his own horses. Lately, he'd been so busy breaking colts for Neal that he hadn't spent enough time with his geldings and mares. He regularly had Shep and Dale take them for rides for exercise, and then let them loose in a pasture so they could graze and enjoy the easy life.

After Boone cinched the lead on the quarter horse he had rescued, he led him to the tack room. Spot followed them, the proud herder, broadcasting that he was available for hire. Boone showed Sofia how he brushed his horse, checked the shoes and saddled him.

"This is Burrito," Boone said by way of introduction.

"You're not serious."

"As a heart attack. I name my horses after my favorite foods."

"And you thought alphabetical order was bad! You won't do that with your children, will you?"

"Nah. Probably not, anyway." He grinned.

"Your wife might have something to say about that."

He felt strangely gratified that she'd mentioned children in front of him without getting a shell-shocked look in her eyes this time.

"You're probably right. Now, would you like to meet Chicken? Okay, I'm kidding. I would never name a horse Chicken. Am I cruel? No." He led out his most gentle horse, a painted black-and-white mare. "This is Oreo. I've bred her once and named the foal Cookie."

"She's beautiful, and that's a perfect name."

The bright sunshine from earlier today took a back seat to a light cloud cover. Earlier in the week, snow had been predicted. Unusual for October in

Montana but entirely possible. Usually, Oreo could smell snow. No one believed Boone, but he'd swear by it. Given that she didn't like snow, Oreo would often try to communicate with him by resistance and an occasional and unusual snort. She'd been right every time. Boone didn't sense any of that today, and after he'd saddled her, Oreo seemed happy to be led out for exercise.

Spot took off after a bird, and Boone handed Sofia Oreo's lead. "Follow me."

Behind him, Boone heard Sofia talking to Oreo. If he wasn't mistaken, she had just complimented Oreo's beautiful mane. Then he heard her speaking in more hushed tones about not being scared, because though she hadn't ridden in a while, she'd always loved horses. Boone wanted to turn and assure Sofia that as an experienced horseman, he'd never allow her to ride an unpredictable horse.

Oreo was a safe, experienced and docile mare. But rather than turn, he continued to listen to her soft, lilting voice, carried slightly by a breeze. His chest pinched when he wondered which one of them Sofia was trying to comfort more. And whether she realized that not everyone talked to horses the way he did. Correction: the way *they* did.

At the end of the lane, he brought the horses together, then came to Sofia's side. "Ready?"

"I think we've gotten acquainted." Sofia smiled up at the horse, and if a horse could smile, Oreo did.

Holding on to Oreo, he offered Sofia his hand. She took it, then reached for the stirrup, easily lifting herself up.

"Do you talk to horses a lot?"

She took the reins in her hands. "This is my first time, I guess. It seemed natural."

Indeed. After giving her a quick reminder lesson on how Oreo would understand her instructions as to which way to go, Boone mounted Burrito.

"You two follow me," he said, then turned Burrito toward the hills.

They started out at an easy trot, but Burrito was clearly itching for more of a ride, so Boone allowed a gallop. Oreo followed, not wanting to be left behind. Occasionally, Boone looked back to check on Sofia. The smile on her face was wide, her cheeks pink. Yeah, she was enjoying this, not thinking about breaking a nail, not thinking about her hair or anything remotely having to do with her looks.

He didn't understand why she was so obsessed with clothes and makeup when she'd been gifted with a natural beauty. She definitely wasn't insecure, but confident and comfortable in her own skin.

Even though the cold air snapped around them, the day was classic Montana. Bright, beautiful, big sky. God's country. He ought to do this more often. Take a ride and figure out the rest of his life. He'd never imagined at thirty-one he'd be back living on his family's ranch. But he'd also never imagined being wealthy like this. His life here had turned out to be much more than he could have expected when he'd only done the right thing and moved here to please his mother.

He thought it would be a short-term situation, but the ranch needed running. And he couldn't complain about his accommodations, or the ability to run the show when it came to anything having to do with the horses. Lastly, his mother reminded him and his brothers that this ranch was *their* legacy and some-day would be their children's legacy.

Ironic that his children, the next generation, would be the ones to gain their land and cattle through inheritance. He was grateful beyond measure to be able to give this to his children and grandchildren someday. The legacy of it all had been the thing to get him thinking more about children. That, and watching both Holt and Morgan settle into their lives as fathers. They weren't anything like Neal had been as a father, and that gave Boone a lot of hope. He, too, could be a different kind of father. Loving. Attentive. And always, always loving and respectful of their mother.

Twenty minutes later, he arrived at the first ridge, and turned to see that Sofia and Oreo had fallen back. He wheeled Burrito around, then headed the short distance back to them.

"I don't know what happened," Sofia said when

he met up with her. "Suddenly Oreo just didn't want to keep going, and she started snorting."

"Oh, boy."

"Was it something I said? I was just telling her about the Mistletoe Rodeo next month. Maybe that was upsetting. Poor baby." She reached to pet Oreo's forelock.

Boone wrinkled his brow, halfway between a laugh and a snort of his own. This woman was constantly surprising him.

"I don't think that's the problem. Believe it or not, it's going to snow."

"Snow? What makes you say that?"

The air was crisp and cold, the leaves bright yellow, orange and red. A typical Montana autumn. But the first snowfall didn't usually hit until November, so this would be unusual.

Sofia listened dumbfounded as Boone told her that Oreo could smell snow in the air before it fell. That she'd proved it time and time again. And Sofia had worried that she'd talked too much about the rodeo. This was an intuitive horse.

"We better head back," Boone advised. "Don't worry. I'm sure we'll get there ahead of the snow."

"How are we going to get her to move?"

But she should have known not to worry. Boone kept them trotting side by side the rest of the way back. To get Oreo to stop resisting, at times he spoke to her, and made little clicking sounds that soothed her. Oreo kept moving, as if she understood Boone's language, and they made it back to the stables as the first snowflakes fell.

Until then, Sofia hadn't believed it would actually snow.

What a weird October. First, a so-called psychic had led her to Boone, a man she'd come to adore. Now, she'd met a horse who could smell snow. What was next? A cow who could sing?

After taking care of the horses and stabling them again, they headed back to the cabin as the snow began to stick to the ground. Spot waited for them at the top step of the wraparound porch, shivering.

Boone picked him up, dusted the snow off his paws, and tucked him in his jacket. "Poor buddy."

Sofia's hands were freezing even inside the leather gloves Boone had handed her in the tack room. She took them off and rubbed her hands together while Boone hauled in some more chopped wood and started another fire.

"Maybe we should wait until it stops snowing before I take you back to your car. It probably won't snow for long."

"Well, since I need a new set of tires, that's probably for the best."

Earlier, Sofia thought that she should go home soon. But this fire, this snowfall, this *man*, had her rethinking everything.

Boone turned to her, jaw gaping. "You need a new set of tires?"

"Just the back ones. It's no big deal. I've been saving, and I didn't think it would snow until at least next month."

"It's dangerous to drive with low tread."

"It's not too bad. Please don't worry."

But he looked concerned, his brow furrowed, and her heart pinched. In the next moment a wallop of pure desire pulsed through her body. She wanted this man more than she'd ever wanted anyone in her life. This was so much more than pure physical attraction.

He straightened. "But I do worry."

She joined him by the crackling fire and went into his arms, which opened easily for her. "I can see that. But I'm safe now, right? No driving in the snow with low tread."

"Are you flirting with me to change the subject?" He palmed the soft hairs on the back of her neck, and that single movement gave her an all-body tingle.

"You might be onto something."

What was it about this man that had such an incredible pull for her? Slowing them down hadn't stopped all these intense feelings. It had only made them stronger. She'd always been a social person, always knew how to work a room and how to party with the best of them.

But with Boone, everything slowed down. She noticed every little nuance of a moment, such as when he took her hand in his and pressed a kiss on the inside of her wrist. When he softly kissed the shell of her ear. When he came up behind her and pulled her back to his chest.

He made time stop.

Boone tipped her chin and smiled. "You are irresistible, you know that?"

"There are worse things to be, right?" She playfully batted her eyelashes.

He met her lips and kissed her, at first tender, then deeper. Longer, stronger and more desperate as the kiss grew in intensity. They broke the kiss only once to stare at each other, and a silent acknowledgment passed between them.

This is crazy. Where have you been all my life? All those silly clichés she'd never thought would apply to her echoed in her mind. Not *her*. She had plans. But it wasn't worth fighting this feeling. It was too good, too powerful.

Sofia reached for him, pulling him down by the nape of his neck to kiss him again and again. Before long she was hot, and it had nothing to do with the roaring fire. She got bold again, pulling his shirt out of his jeans. Her fingers drifted up and down his sinewy, strong back. He squeezed her behind and groaned.

Then he took a step back. "Tell me one thing first. Why did you *really* want to slow us down?"

She didn't have to think long to come up with her answer. "*This*. Us. We're explosive. Combustible."

"And that's a bad thing?" He cocked his head. "Be honest with me."

"It scares me," she admitted. "I've always been in control. This has never happened to me before with any guy. With you, I lose my head."

And I'm afraid I'll lose my heart.

"Baby, believe me, I get that. More than you know. But you've thought about us now, and you're sure?"

He needed to hear the words from her, and she respected him even more for that.

"I'm sure I want this. I want *you*. I want it all. Everything you want to give me."

He flashed her a wicked smile, then in one swift move threw her over his shoulder and began walking up the staircase.

"That fire is for you, Spot. Enjoy."

It was very he-man and alpha of him to carry her over his shoulder like a conquest, but she wasn't going to argue. This was hot, and it also gave her a wonderful view of his incredible butt. He kicked the door open, and she stopped staring at his butt and tried to get a first impression view of his bedroom. First, it shouldn't be called a *bedroom*. It was the size of some apartments and probably three times the size of her studio.

He set her down, and that's when she took a good look around. Boone actually had a fireplace in his bedroom. Interesting to witness the way the other half lived.

"A *fireplace*?" She nudged her chin in the direction of the hearth, covered in masonry stones.

"You want a fire?"

"Yes," she said, then plastered her body against his. Hip to hip, they continued to kiss and ravish each other's mouths. It was all the fire she needed.

Boone did his magic again, going after the soft shell of her ear, his calloused fingers against the silky hairs on her neck. When he nibbled at her earlobe, she trembled with longing. Then those hands were under her sweater, making her quiver. She raised her arms when Boone pulled her sweater off, revealing the push-up bra she'd worn today. Not having planned any of this, it was pumpkin orange with black trim, but at least it matched her panties.

She bit back a smile when Boone took it all in. "Happy Halloween."

"*Dayum*, baby. You even make orange look sexy." His finger traced the strap of her bra before he gently unhooked it, then covered her nipple with his mouth.

"Boone," she moaned, and clutched his head as his tongue revved her up in seconds.

She almost didn't realize that she was being moved until suddenly they were beside the bed on the other side of the room. So she pushed him down on the bed, enjoying when he tumbled easily and pulled her down with him.

He rolled them and pinned her under his hard body, threading their hands together and raising them above her head.

"Got you right where I want you," he whispered.

"Exactly where I want to be."

She would now stop overanalyzing their connection. A strange mix of good fortune and contentment sank all the way to her soul.

Boone kissed down the column of her neck to the dip in her shoulder, and unleashed his skilled tongue to touch and explore every part of her flesh. He never missed a spot, the overachiever. Trying to keep up, she arched against him. He groaned and released her hands from his grip, going after her pants, tugging at the waistline.

"Lift up," he instructed, and she obliged, planting her feet and raising her butt while he slid her leggings off.

She shimmied and he lowered, finally revealing her matching panties.

Trick or treat, she nearly said, but decided "Happy Halloween" had been cheesy enough.

"Trick or treat?" he said, and she wondered if he read minds.

Or maybe just hers.

"Nice." He trailed the leg seam of her panties, obviously admiring the high cut instead of their color.

"I'm not dressed for seduction."

"You could wear a cloth sack and I'd still find

you gorgeous." He pressed a warm kiss on her upper thigh, then pulled on her panties until they were off.

She lay there, naked, while his hot gaze swept over her with a slow smile.

"C'mon, slacker! Clothes off." She sat up, tugged on his belt, managing to unbuckle it. "Join me, why don't you."

"Yes, ma'am," he said, while unbuttoning his shirt with excruciating precision. "We're going slow this time. Not like our first time. Don't rush me."

Chapter Fourteen

A long while later, Sofia lay sated under a pile of blankets, her legs entwined with Boone's, her head in the crook of his shoulder. He'd been playing with her hair, then made a move to disentangle.

She tightened her legs. "Don't go."

"Just going to start a fire."

"Oh, that *would* be cozy. Sure, I'll allow it."

"Thank you, baby." He chuckled, pressed a kiss to her shoulder and climbed out of bed.

Pulling his boxer briefs on, Boone went out the bedroom door and came back a few minutes later with a load of firewood. She watched as the muscles in his arms and back bunched, more shocking evidence that some men looked far better wearing no clothes at all. He proceeded to arrange the wood and kindling and she went up on both elbows with fascination. Boone Dalton was the real thing. A mountain man. Her cowboy.

And what a man. He could make a woman's toes curl, talk to horses, adopt stray dogs and make a fire look pretty damn hot while making it. Why had *she never fallen for a cowboy before?* She couldn't think of a single reason except that she hadn't known what she was missing. Jeans, leather and boots were definitely the way to go.

Boone caught her staring and smiled. "What?"

"Oh, just enjoying the view."

"You'll enjoy this fire in a few minutes." He tossed the kindling inside, then stacked the wood and threw in a lit match. In no time the fire roared to life, the flames licking and crackling.

Outside, a light snow continued to fall, turning the daylight into dull shades of gray.

Boone looked out the window. "It's actually not too bad out there. I'm thinking about dinner. I should tell you that we can't get a pizza delivered out here. Especially not in this weather."

"Food does sound good. But please come back to bed, cowboy."

He rolled on top of her, tucking her next to him.

In the crook between his neck and the dip of his shoulder, she stroked the light smattering of hairs on his chest. "I was just remembering how Winona Cobbs told me to pick your entry."

"You mean it wasn't my brothers' great writing that made you pick me?"

"Sure, but it was just strange the way she specifically pointed to your blue envelope. She said, 'This is the one.'"

"Well, I'm going to have to thank her personally someday." Boone tugged her closer, pressing a kiss to her temple. "Even if I didn't need the clothes, I needed you."

The sweet words wrapped around her heart, warm and intimate. "That's just it. I thought it was weird once I found out that you didn't even want the clothes. I mean, what kind of a psychic is she?"

"She might not be a psychic, but maybe she's my fairy godmother." Boone chuckled.

Sofia stopped short of telling Boone that she'd heard Winona apparently considered it her duty to teach the young people of Bronco not to be too busy with their lives to miss finding love. But maybe the feelings Sofia had right now, strong though they were, would fade. This might be the first time she'd ever fallen in love, but though Boone was her first love, he still might not be her *true* love. Her one and only with lasting power. Only time would tell.

You're not ready for that, anyway.

Her inner voice was right. But Camilla had been right, too. Falling in love was…delicious.

Boone's phone buzzed, and he picked it up from the nightstand beside him. "I guess I should check this."

They'd both heard the phone buzzing earlier and ignored it due to their more, ahem, pressing concerns. Boone's eyes widened and he sat up ramrod straight.

"What? What's going on?"

He ran a hand down his face. "Just let me get rid of her."

Oh well, *this* didn't sound good! Get rid of whom?

Unwelcome jealousy spiked through her. Some old girlfriend might have shown up out of the blue. Unable to let him go. And who could really blame anyone who wanted to a second chance with Boone Dalton?

"Who?" She couldn't help but ask him.

"My mother. She said she's been calling me and saw my truck so she's heading on over. She's got dinner for me." Boone shoved on his shirt and pulled up his jeans. "I'd like you to meet her, but maybe this isn't the best time."

Sofia sat up and smoothed down her hair. "No, definitely not."

Boone cocked his head. "I mean, you're naked, and I would like to keep you that way a little longer. I'm selfish that way."

He shut the bedroom door, and Sofia settled back under the covers. As long as the snow continued to fall and Boone continued to hold her, she didn't want to go anywhere at all. But it was Sunday, and her parents would be expecting her unless she called them.

She picked up her phone to dial, and her mother answered. "Are we seeing Boone again tonight?" Denise Sanchez asked without preamble.

"I'm actually not coming over. Remember my tires? I think maybe I should just…stay put." She didn't want to lie and say she was at her apartment. They'd probably come and get her.

"What will you eat for dinner?"

"Believe it or not, I can cook for myself."

"Oh, *mija*." Her mother's tone said: poor, poor, delusional Sofia.

"I'm serious!" Well, she could microwave a frozen entrée, anyway.

"Well, it's odd. Camilla called to say she's not coming over, either. It's only a light dusting of snow. You both act as if you weren't raised in Montana."

Sofia briefly wondered if Camilla and Jordan were doing the same kind of cuddling that she'd been enjoying with Boone. It wouldn't surprise her. After all, they were newlyweds.

"It's just a nice day to stay home and get cozy under the covers."

"I'd come and get you myself, but I heard that your thermostat was fixed. So I won't worry."

"I'm fine. Perfectly toasty and warm." She stared at the roaring fire. Nothing but the truth.

Sofia hung up, having dispensed all her familial obligations. In no hurry to get her car, or get back into her clothes, she buried herself under the covers. Now all she needed was Boone, and whatever home-cooked dinner his mother had brought over for him.

Boone ran down the steps and found Spot already sniffing at the front door as if he could smell a newcomer. He swung open the door in time to see his mother coming up the porch steps carrying a bag. Behind her was the golf cart she used to occasionally get around the ranch to her sons' different cabins. Barefoot, he hopped over the ice-cold walkway and closed the distance between them, taking the bag from her. Spot did his yappy and yippy thing at the door but wisely stayed inside.

"What are you doing? You didn't have to bring dinner. I could have come over to pick it up. It's snowing."

"Really? I hadn't noticed." She stepped inside the foyer, dressed like a hardy ranch wife, in snow boots, a Western hat and a blue parka that came to her ankles. "Why are you barefoot?"

"When you texted, I was…upstairs. I just took a…um, a shower."

Damn, he'd never been able to lie to his mother. Not convincingly, anyway.

"Uh-huh. And why isn't your hair wet?"

"I didn't wash it." As if he was still eight and caught in an obvious lie, Boone still couldn't give up. He just kept digging his own grave with a plastic spoon.

"You're no better at this than you were as a child." She shook her head and pursed her lips in mock disapproval. "Holt told me what happened at the Harvest Festival earlier. You two left very suddenly."

His darn brother, snitching on Boone. "Okay, well, if you're worried, Sofia is fine. No damages.

I just brought her here so she could wash up. It was closer than her apartment."

"Right." His mother looked behind him. "Is she still here?"

Good grief. He didn't answer, then she surprised him. She reached over and took the bag from him.

"Hey!"

"I decided you should come over for dinner tonight. I can't actually remember the last time you made dinner with the family. Holt and Morgan come by semi-regularly with their kids."

She'd conveniently forgotten that Morgan hadn't always joined them for dinner, either, before he'd met his new bride. Before he and Neal had reconciled.

"Is this your way of inviting Sofia to dinner with the family?"

"If she's here, then yes."

"Great, *if* she's here, I'll invite her."

"Fine, and if she's not, I do still expect to at least see *you* for dinner. I've been wrong allowing you to stay away from your father. I think it's called enabling. Reconciliation between you two is long past overdue." She pointed her index finger at him. "Dinner is in thirty minutes. A prime rib roast and my creamy mashed potatoes, your favorite."

With that she turned to get back on the cart and took herself and her dinner back down the hill.

Boone shut the door. So close and yet so far. He could still smell the delicious prime rib that had been in his hands seconds ago. His fantasies of eating in bed with Sofia, or in front of the fire, were squashed like a bug. When he made his way back upstairs, the most gorgeous woman in the world was pulling pants on past her curvy behind.

"What are you doing?"

"Your mother was downstairs. I can't be naked when your mother is in the house!"

"It's not like she has X-ray vision."

"You don't know that! Well, okay, she doesn't have X-ray vision, but she has mother's intuition! That's a dangerous thing." She took a breath. "Did you leave the food downstairs?"

He came to her side, pulling her into his arms, and inhaled her light and sweet scent. "I'm afraid she changed her mind and invited us to dinner tonight instead."

She blinked. "Does she know I'm here?"

"She suspects. I swear *she's* the one who's really psychic."

"It's that mom's intuition thing, I'm telling you!"

"I had wanted you to meet the rest of my family. My two idiot brothers. My mother. She's a sweet woman when she's minding her own business. I swear." He smoothed back her wild mane of hair.

Personally, he loved this look on her. Those tight stretchy pants and a sweater. Her hair in the decidedly tousled look she seemed to like so much on him. He loved that he was the one responsible for that rumpled and tangled hair, as if he'd branded her. Changed her.

Made her his own.

"Boone, I can't meet the rest of your family tonight. I have no clothes!"

"What do you mean? You're wearing them."

She gave him a "men are so hopeless" stare. "You saw how I dressed for dinner at my folks'. I wouldn't want to give your family anything less than my best."

"And you think your best has to do with the clothes you wear?"

"Presentation *matters*."

"I know, you've said that. But I don't believe it. You're not that shallow."

"Boone," she said, sounding like he'd wounded her.

But they were going to have this talk. Fully clothed and therefore a lot more clearheaded, he walked her back to the bed, sat and pulled her into his arms.

"I don't mean to hurt your feelings, Sofia. But tell me why all this means so much to you. There's a lot more to it than you let on."

"What makes you think that?"

It did seem odd, but some days, he could almost read her thoughts. At times, he strangely felt that he knew her better than he knew himself.

"Because I know you, and you have a lot more to offer than a beautiful, as you put it, presentation."

"I don't want to bother you with this. It's nothing,

really." But her shoulders lowered. "I know I seem totally confident all the time, and I really am."

"But…?"

She pulled away from him and stared at the hands she'd folded on her lap. "I don't even think Camilla knows about this. I never told her, or anyone else. Growing up in a family with five children, you can imagine money was tight. My parents did the best they could, but I wore Camilla's hand-me-downs. I remember feeling so beautiful because I got to wear the dresses and outfits my big sister wore until she gave them to me. She took good care of them. Whenever she'd get a particularly nice outfit, I counted the days until she grew out of it. I had a favorite dress, a blue-and-yellow one that had been washed so much it slipped on me like a piece of silk." She hesitated and ran a hand over her face. "Oh boy, this is so stupid."

He tugged her hand away. "No, it's not. Tell me."

"I was in fifth grade when I first wore that dress to school feeling like a princess. Really working the dress, you know? It fit me perfectly, and I loved wearing it. And then one of the mean girls came up to me and said the dress had looked better on Camilla. Why couldn't I get my own clothes and stop being such a copycat? Was I poor, or what?"

The image of a young Sofia feeling hurt and embarrassed for wearing hand-me-downs made his stomach tight as a fist. "I hope you told that girl where she could stick it."

She laughed. "Something like that. That was the beginning of my realization that style is something you're born with. Not always something you can put on like a coat. And that's exactly what I told that girl. That I felt sorry for her because she needed new clothes for style, and I made every outfit my own. But I told myself that when I got older and could afford to buy my own clothes, I'd always have only the best."

"All I can tell you, baby, is that my family is not going to judge you."

"Yeah, I know. Good people never do. Maybe I've let my love for fashion take over my life too much. I don't know. You reminded me of that little girl, and that style isn't always about clothes. You, Boone Dalton, have the kind of style that money can't buy."

"Yeah?"

"You *own* it. You don't apologize for who you are. Even if you're wearing a simple pair of jeans and cowboy boots that I've seen a million times before."

"Thank you, but this is about you." He cupped her face with his palms and looked into her brown eyes. "What happened to that little girl who had her own style and didn't need any fancy clothes to show it?"

"She's in there, but has a better clothing allowance now."

He chuckled. "Are you okay going to dinner, or do I have to make an excuse?"

"I'm fine. Like you, I'll just have to work what I'm wearing."

Then it hit him. This confident woman, this beauty that he'd never seen the slightest bit insecure, was worried about meeting his folks.

"You're nervous." He tugged on a lock of her hair.

"I want them to like me."

"They're going to love you. Are you kidding?" He studied her. "I mean, you've met Cornelius. Even you told me that my dad isn't half as bad as him."

"Yeah, well, maybe when I met Cornelius, I didn't *care* what he thought of me."

"Another way in which we're alike. You notice there are a lot of those ways, right?"

"You do seem to have every song on my playlist."

The words hardly needed to be said, but it was always good to speak the truth.

"I probably don't need to say this, I mean, I hope I've made myself clear from the moment I met you. Because this isn't business as usual for me. You and I, we're…we started something real, and it means a lot to me. I'm not fooling around. I love you, Sofia. I can't believe it happened so fast but there it is. Now, you can run away from me, or you can just see where this goes."

As he stared into her stunned dark eyes, he calculated whether she would bolt now, or not until after dinner. If she made that choice, best that she did it now and he could avoid a greater heartache later.

Instead, she blinked a few times, smiled and cupped his jaw.

"I've fallen in love with you, and it feels pretty wonderful. It's the first time for me."

He reached for her hand and pressed a kiss to her palm. "Man, do I feel lucky."

Chapter Fifteen

It was official. Boone's older brother, Morgan, was the most like him.

Morgan had also claimed to fall in love at first sight with Erica. Boone never thought it would happen to him, but he'd now come to terms with the fact that he hadn't been the same man since the moment he met Sofia. She'd wound herself around his heart without even trying. Plenty of beautiful women had come after him in the past, professing their undying love and devotion, even before the money windfall. But never anyone like Sofia. He knew without a doubt that there could never be anyone else for him.

After they'd both cleaned up a little, Boone grabbed the golf cart he kept in the barn behind his stables for the short ride to the main house. The distance between the homes made for a good walk, but not in this weather. He'd walk or ride a horse, but he didn't want either Sofia *or* Burrito to get too cold. Bundled up in jackets and hats, he drove with Sofia, her hand on his thigh.

Her head turned to admire the hills and mountains dotted with snow. "So pretty out here."

The snow had let up, but considering the sun had set, none of it had melted away. It wouldn't last long on the ground, and in terms of Montana snowfalls, this one was an infant. They'd get a true snowstorm for the first time next month, and likely a white Christmas, too. He looked forward to spending many days in his warm bed with Sofia.

Erica greeted them at the door, holding little Josie. "Hey, you two! Glad to see you again. What's it been, a few hours?"

He didn't take his hand off Sofia's lower back, guiding her through the entryway and toward the stone hearth with another roaring fire. Holt, Morgan, Shep and Dale were gathered in front of it.

Morgan turned from where he'd been poking at a log, and his face lit up when Erica rejoined him, as if she hadn't only been gone for a few seconds. And to think Boone, Thing 1 and Thing 2 used to make fun of him privately. Speaking of his younger brothers, introductions were finally made between Sofia and the two people who'd underhandedly orchestrated their first meeting.

"These are the two bozos who wrote the letter that played on your heartstrings. Meet Shep, over there. He's the short one."

"Hey!" Shep said, but smiled. He was around six feet or so, only a little shorter than Boone.

"And that's Dale. He's the funny-looking one."

Then his mother bustled in the room and offered her hand. "Hi, I'm Deborah."

"Nice to meet you. I'm Sofia Sanchez."

"I know your mother, Mrs. Sanchez. She cuts my hair on a regular basis." Deborah briefly touched her hair.

"What? You didn't tell me that," Boone said.

"I don't tell you everything, honey."

"And you've already met my father, Neal Dalton." Boone introduced them without looking at Neal.

"Yes, we've met. How are you, Mr. Dalton?" Sofia asked with the smoothness of someone used to dealing with difficult men.

"Good, good. Nice to see you again." Neal lazily put a hand around Deborah's shoulders.

"Everything's ready," his mother said. "Let's go sit down."

She led them to the dining room with the twelve-person farm table. The place setting looked as if it were already the holidays. Boone hadn't eaten at this table since last Christmas, but he knew his parents held dinner here at least once a week, though not always on a Sunday. Lately he'd made his excuses—too much work, problem with a horse—and Mom brought him leftovers. Apparently, that might be over now, and he'd need to sit with Neal or risk no more home-cooked meals.

As they ate and chatted about the first snowfall,

Boone watched his father. He sat at the head of the table, a place Boone wasn't certain he deserved. His mother should be there, the woman who'd single-handedly kept their little family together while Neal had been off gambling, drinking and…well, his mind didn't want to go there. Because of her, and her alone, they were still a family.

He *wanted* to forgive Neal. Carrying around all this resentment inside wasn't hurting anyone but Boone. Clearly, Neal continued to be unaffected by the fact that not all of his sons had forgiven him. As long as he had his wife, and she'd forgiven him, he seemed satisfied. But if that were true, would Neal still be trying to do something nice for Boone? If only it didn't feel like his father was trying to buy Boone's forgiveness.

"So, tell us how you two met," his mother said. "I want to hear the whole story, Boone."

"For that, you should ask Dale and Shep," Boone said, his arm draped around Sofia.

Sofia smiled. "He won a contest."

"We thought Boone could use a new wardrobe, so we entered him in that drawing BH Couture was having," Shep piped in. "It was funny. Admit it."

"That how you met Sofia? Through the contest you won?" Mom gaped.

"She was the stylist fitting me with the new ward-robe." Still not quite believing his good fortune, Boone inched closer to her.

"I didn't think he would actually win," Dale said, taking a heap of mashed potatoes. "Guess I'm *that* good."

"We explained in the letter how much Boone needed a new wardrobe, because we all know that he does," Shep said. "He has one pair of boots that he uses until they wear out."

"Good grief, Shep," Mrs. Dalton said.

"It was a good letter." Sofia squeezed Boone's thigh.

"We didn't write anything that wasn't true," Dale said. "We're not spending like those lottery winners who lose it all in the first year. And we're ranchers, especially Boone."

"What do you mean, especially Boone?" Morgan said. "I know my way around the ranch."

"Take it easy," Boone joked.

"I think it's kismet," his mother said. "Destiny. Would you like to hear how Neal and I met? I went to my first rodeo, where I got stood up by a blind date. Neal said the same thing had happened to him. He asked whether I'd like to join him for the day, so my first rodeo wouldn't be a total waste. We were both there anyway, right? Turns out Neal *had* no date. He just wanted to spend the day with me. And the rest is history."

"Dad, you sly dog," Morgan said.

"We've all heard this story about a million times," Holt said, taking the butter knife away from Robby.

"I saw a beautiful woman that I wanted to get to know better," Neal said. "She didn't know a doggone thing about the rodeo. I walked around pointing, 'that's a horse, that's a bull.' Really, it was almost that bad."

"Oh, Neal! You're exaggerating." His mother playfully swatted her husband. "True, I didn't know much about the rodeo, or ranch life, for that matter. But after that day, my life certainly changed. For the better. It was meant to be."

"Kismet," his father said, cutting into his prime rib.

Guess Boone wasn't the only man in his family who'd ever lied to a woman just to get a chance to know her.

For a long time, Boone had a vision in his mind of marrying a woman just like his mother. Someone devoted to her family. Yet he'd fallen for Sofia, a woman so different from her. Yet there was something to be said for a woman like Sofia, who wouldn't put up with the kind of crap his mother had over the years. Loyalty and devotion would only go so far to save a rocky marriage. His parents were lucky. The gambling windfall had certainly gone a long way to ease tensions. And his mother's heart attack had been a wake-up call.

But if Boone ever treated Sofia badly, if he ever lied to her again, she'd be gone in a second. He respected that and wouldn't have it any other way.

* * *

Sofia wondered if the Daltons had prime rib every week. At the Sanchez house, that dish was reserved for once a year, on either Christmas Eve or New Year's Day. Then again, from everything she'd seen, this was the home of bona fide cattle ranchers. And despite their wealth, they weren't particularly showy about it. The home was large but homey. These were down-to-earth people that were still adjusting to their windfall.

Dale, the "funny-looking" brother, was almost as strikingly good-looking as Boone. Heck, all of the brothers were. She'd wondered where they got their looks, because Neal wasn't quite as handsome. Tall, yes. Imposing. Almost a little scary. But she'd gotten her answer when a beautiful blonde had waltzed in the room.

Deborah Dalton wore a pageboy hairstyle and looked a little like an older Grace Kelly. Classy. Though all of the brothers took after their father with brown hair, Boone had his mother's riveting blue eyes, a deep indigo. And speaking of style, Deborah wore jeans and a long-sleeved blue peasant top. Nothing extraordinary, but she wore it like a model on a runaway, exuding confidence and assuredness. So similar to the way Boone carried himself. Sofia liked her immediately.

Deborah obviously straddled both worlds, and Sofia could just as easily picture her leading a corporate boardroom meeting as hosting a dinner as a wealthy rancher's wife. The matriarch of five boys, she was clearly adored by each one of her sons. But it was nothing compared to the way that Neal doted on his wife. Sofia thought it verged on the ridiculous, but extremely sweet.

Still, she could feel the tension practically coming off Boone in waves anytime Neal said a word.

Forgive. I'm not good at that.

That much was clear. She felt bad for Boone. Life was too short for regrets and for withholding love. She wished she could do something to bridge the gap between father and son. But she had a feeling it would have to be a significant emotional event to get Boone to forgive Neal. Someday, for the sake of them both, she hoped it would happen.

Later, after dessert, which turned out to be a two-layer chocolate cake with raspberry filling, Holt and Amanda excused themselves, saying that Robby had a strict bedtime. Morgan and Erica, too, left soon after, because Josie had begun to fuss. Other than that, Sofia was surprised at how well behaved the children had been through dinner.

"Coffee, anyone?" Deborah rolled her eyes at her husband. "Don't worry, I have my decaf."

"Let me help you."

Sofia followed Deborah to the kitchen, listening in the background as Boone and his two younger brothers talked smack about fake Tinder profiles and whose turn it was to muck the stalls.

"Those boys of mine," Deborah said. "They're always playing practical jokes on one another. But none of them has ever resulted in my meeting a lovely young lady."

Sofia smiled. "Thank you. You know, your family reminds me of my own in many ways."

"Oh, really?"

"Large and loud. I feel right at home."

"It's kind of you to say that. Your mother was equally welcoming, very down-to-earth and warm to everyone. But I know that my husband isn't well liked in town. That's because they don't know him. Just wait until they all find out he's one of the smartest businessmen I've ever met. Completely self-taught."

Sofia didn't think it appropriate to mention the schism between Boone and his father. Deborah was well aware, and Sofia had nothing to add in terms of solving the problem. Together, they prepared the coffee, Sofia grinding the fresh beans and loading the coffee maker while Deborah brought out the china cups and saucers.

"Oh, how I miss my coffee," Deborah said with a slight shake of her head. "It used to make me buzz around the house for hours. I got so much done in those days."

"I'm sorry to hear about your heart attack."

"Thank you, but though I've got a clean bill of health from the cardiologist, you wouldn't know it by looking at my husband. He really is going to have to calm down and realize I'm not going anywhere. I'm not breakable."

"You don't look breakable." In fact, she reminded Sofia of her own mother, someone who hadn't taken a single sick day in a decade.

"My heart attack scared them. Heck, it scared me, too. Life is too short to hold on to anger and resentments. I've vowed never to go to bed angry with any of my loved ones."

"I admire that attitude."

"Listen, I'm sure you've noticed that Boone and his father aren't on the best of terms. But don't judge him for that. Boone is just overprotective of me. My husband and I had some tough times, and the boys always sided with me. Boone, he's always been the proverbial middle child. Our peacemaker. Whenever the brothers had a fight, you would see Boone getting in the middle, taking the hit if he had to. He loves his brothers, no matter how much they tease one another and play pranks."

"My brothers are the same way."

"How many do you have?"

"Three. And one sister."

"At least your mother had two girls. I'm so grateful for Josie, and I hope that my boys will give me more granddaughters. I'd love to reestablish the gender balance in the Dalton family."

The way Holt and Amanda, not to mention Morgan and Erica, stole sultry looks at each other all through dinner, Sofia would bet there'd be another Dalton coming along soon enough.

"Robby sure is all boy," Sofia said.

"He sure is." The coffee brewed and Deborah began to pour some into the cups. "He reminds me a lot of both Boone and Holt when they were that age. So busy, so active."

"What was Boone like as a little boy?" She could almost picture him now, a mischievous smile, those adorable dimples.

"In trouble a lot." Deborah laughed and glanced up from the pouring. "But he always took care of his brothers. At school, Boone was always the one in the middle of a fight defending whichever kid was being picked on that day. He'd always wind up with a shiner himself. And lord forbid anyone who went after his brothers!"

Sofia laughed, thinking of how he referred to his brothers as Thing 1 and Thing 2. And because of them, she'd had a chance to meet Boone. Otherwise, she wondered if they would have ever met. At least, not in the way they did, because he would have never walked into her shop otherwise.

"I honestly never thought that boy would settle

down, but then Neal bought him his first horse. And nothing was the same after that. He found his focus."

"It was Neal who did that?" Sofia took one of the cups and saucers and placed it on the tray Deborah had on the counter.

"Ironic, isn't it? They were close when the boys were little. All of them were. Neal was a good horseman for most of his life, but he admits that he's no match for Boone."

The thought that his father had introduced Boone to his passion would have maybe carried more weight at another time. Now Boone hardly seemed to acknowledge it.

The conversation between Sofia and Boone's mother was so smooth and easy that Sofia almost felt like she did in her own mother's kitchen.

That is, without all the teasing about her relationship status. Then she wondered what Deborah would think once she realized that Sofia had fallen in love with her son.

Maybe then there would be two mothers waiting for grandchildren.

One on each side.

Later, Boone drove Sofia to get her car. The snow had lightly covered the hood, and Boone brushed it off. She would have no trouble driving home.

"Thank you for dinner, and…everything else,"

Sofia said as they kissed one last time, remembering "everything else."

"Text me when you get in, or I'll worry about those tires." Boone pulled his huge jacket tight around her, then pressed his forehead to hers. "And remember that I love you."

"I love you, too."

Sofia drove home, a sense of giddiness enveloping her. As she turned on the road leading her back to Bronco Valley, she felt caught between two places. She was still the same old Sofia, but falling in love with Boone made her feel…new. It was like being caught between two opposing views. The old Sofia wanted to warn the new Sofia that this was all happening too soon. Too quickly. Love grew with time. It didn't just sprout up one day fully formed. Right?

Gosh, she didn't know. The feelings were unfamiliar and a little overwhelming. She hadn't planned for this at all. First, she was supposed to get her career established. Then, at one point, she'd meet "the one." She and her man would date for two years, realize they were in love, and have a long engagement, followed by a lovely wedding.

She had already accepted that she couldn't move away from Bronco, as her family would be devastated. But there would be frequent trips to New York City for Fashion Week and the like. She definitely wanted a big life that involved more than Bronco, Montana. Somehow, she'd veered wildly off plan.

By the time Sofia arrived at her apartment, she was hyperventilating.

She nearly knocked her own door down in a hurry to get inside her apartment to something familiar. Comforting. She was a different person than the one who'd left here earlier today, and it felt a bit like whiplash.

After changing into her jammies, Sofia curled up in front of the TV. First, she texted Boone that she'd arrived okay. Next, she texted Camilla:

Help! I think I'm in love.

Chapter Sixteen

Lately whenever Sofia wanted to see Camilla, she'd head to the Library. After her panicked text on Sunday night, Camilla suggested this couldn't be a conversation held over the phone. So it was dinner out, Monday night, just the two of them, as long as they could eat at her new restaurant. Sofia had heard all the statistics straight from Camilla: most restaurants failed in the first five years. And Camilla was determined to be a success. This meant she practically lived at the Library.

Camilla's restaurant was in Bronco Valley, at the location of the town's former abandoned library. Last year Camilla had devised a business plan and found a silent partner, and the old building had been completely renovated. Considering that every time Sofia had been here there was a line out the door, she figured business was going well. She was so proud of her sister, working hard and achieving her dreams. She'd always been such a good example for Sofia and she'd helped Sofia put together a business plan, too.

Only Sofia hadn't done much searching for an investor. She still felt far away from that step. Her port-folio and book of design sketches would only take her so far if she never shared them with anyone who could help. Like Alexis. And yes, maybe she'd been dragging her feet on that end, enjoying the creation part far more than the business aspect. Unlike Camilla, Sofia didn't have a head for business. Unlike Camilla, Sofia had never taken business courses.

As a designer she could sell her sketches to a major design label before she ever created her own brand. She could get started right at BH Couture, with Alexis. Maybe that was the way to go, but open-ing up a bridal shop like Vera Wang had started out might be the better option to begin. Still, she would need investors for that.

"You have to try the potato skins," Camilla said from across the table. "Rafael really outdid himself with those."

When the waitress came by, Camilla ordered for them both. "Now, why are you freaking out about finally falling in love?"

"Everything is happening so fast with me and Boone, and I didn't plan for any of this."

"You fell in love. It's about time it happened to you, but that's not something that can be planned."

"But by the time you fell for Jordan, you were ready to start your restaurant."

"So what? We're sisters, but think about how dif-ferent we are. You've always been confident, and I used to struggle believing in myself. Worrying that if I tried when I wasn't entirely sure of myself and my strategy, I would fail. You dress like a model half the time, and I still dress like a teenager. Our lives are not going to be the same. You're lucky that you found Boone while you're still young. What about people who wait forever and never find the one for them? Think of poor Winona! She had to spend her whole life away from the man she loved, *and* their child."

Just the idea that Sofia would be separated from Boone for decades sent little tremors of fear running through her.

"But I still feel so far behind on my dreams. And I can't let anything or *anyone* derail me."

"Then don't let him."

"But I love him. He's my first love. Why did he have to show up at the wrong time? Why did I have to meet the perfect man right now?"

"Hmm," Camilla said. "Maybe the fact that the timing is all wrong says that he's not the right man?"

"No, he's the *perfect* man for me. But I wish I was…ready for him."

"What is it that you're really afraid of? How can he derail your dreams unless you let him?"

It was a good question. Maybe because falling in love this hard had already changed her. Picturing spending the rest of her life with Boone felt like everything she'd ever wanted. It didn't scare her or make her want to run. But she worried that she'd change a little bit more every year, and pretty soon she wouldn't even recognize the woman she'd become. Then she'd look back on her life and be sorry that she hadn't pursued her dreams.

"What if he wants marriage and children sooner than I do? Believe me, he's ready! Does that mean that I have to give him up? I don't want to lose him, but is that fair to him?"

"Oh, boy. I've never seen you like this before." Camilla patted her hand. "It's going to be okay. Look, if he loves you, he's going to give you all the time you need. Remember what happened with Jordan. He gave me the space I asked for so that I could be sure, and he didn't go anywhere. If it's real love, it will last through some minor disagreements on the way to happily-ever-after."

Sofia left the Library feeling so much better about everything. Boone wouldn't rush her. He'd already proved that by giving her a few days of space when she'd said she wanted to slow them down. When she was ready to resume their relationship, he was there. He understood her better than anyone else, so of course he would understand that she wanted to wait for marriage and children.

The next day, she texted Boone her good morning as usual, along with all the heart emojis, then got ready to leave for work. It wasn't until she walked up to her car that she noticed something markedly

different. Clearly, her back tires had been replaced.
They were sparkling clean and had that bright white
mark. She walked alongside the car, and yep, the
front tires were new also.

She shook her head. "Oh, Boone."

One thing she loved was that he always gifted
her with things that she needed and didn't send ge-
neric gifts like flowers and candy. She pulled out her
phone to text him:

Thank you for the tires. xo

He replied:

You saw that. You're welcome. I didn't want to worry
anymore.

She'd nearly saved all the money already, so she'd
catch him on her next paycheck. She would always
expect to pull her own weight, even if her boyfriend
was a millionaire. But it was nice that he wanted to
take care of her.

Her day at work went smoothly, and she styled
another male customer in some of the clothes he'd
seen Boone wear in the photo shoot.

"I'd like the Boone Works," he said, and Sofia had
become used to the term by now. "There's a woman,
and I'm getting up the courage to ask her out."

"Good for you. They say clothes make the man."

But not always, as she'd found. Some cowboys were perfect just the way they were.

Alexis was happy, their customers were happy, and Sofia was happy. Any moment now little bluebirds would start singing and help her put the clothes away.

"Wow, you're in a good mood," Alexis said. "Is it because of Boone?"

"Yeah, we're getting along." She hesitated to spill her guts to Alexis, because she'd always kept her personal life separate from work.

Another thing had changed in Sofia since she'd fallen for Boone. She had a lot more faith in her sketches, and she honestly wondered why she'd waited so long to talk to Alexis about her ideas. Maybe now was the right time. When there was a lull in customers, Sofia steeled herself and took a deep breath. She went to her car and pulled out the lovely leather-bound case that contained her portfolio of sketches. Some of these she'd been working on since she was away at college.

"Alexis, do you have a minute?"

"Sure, what's up?" Alexis looked up from the catalog of couture designer lines that she regularly purchased from. She was already looking at the spring lines.

"I would love your advice."

"Say yes!"

"Huh?"

"The minute Boone asks you to get hitched, say yes in the next breath, and become Mrs. Filthy-Rich Cowboy. Then have plenty of his babies."

You're as bad as my mother.

Sofia gulped. "That's…not what I wanted advice about."

"Honey, I'm just kidding." She waved dismissively. "That's what I'd do, but then again, you're not me. What can I do for you?"

Even if those comments had thrown Sofia, she handed over her portfolio. "These are some of my ideas. You might remember that I received my fashion design degree from Montana State. I would really love your input."

Considering it had taken Sofia three years to come up with the nerve to share her work with Alexis, this was a watershed moment. Do or die. She reminded herself that Alexis wasn't the only person she respected in this field. If Alexis didn't appreciate Sofia's work, there were other contacts. But at least she'd taken the first in possibly a long line of steps. Her fingers trembled with anticipation. In a few minutes, she would know whether Alexis believed that she had any kind of talent.

Alexis pulled out the first sketch, briefly glanced at it, then suddenly stood up. "Are you not happy here? I don't want to lose you, Sofia! You're my best stylist."

"What? No, I love it here. I'm not going anywhere."

Alexis went hand over heart. "Oh. Okay. Thank you."

"So, what do you think?"

She sat, pulled out a few more sketches, and looked them over. "You have a real eye, that's for sure. I'm not at all surprised. If you'd like to someday design for one of the lines, well, I have some contacts for you to get started. It might take a while, because it's a tough business, as you know, but it's a start."

"Thank you, Alexis. That's all I can ask of you. It means a lot to me."

"Of course, honey."

She wanted to text Boone immediately and tell him what she'd done. She felt nearly giddy with excitement. But this was something she should tell him in person, maybe over a bottle of champagne.

A while later, Sofia stood behind the counter counting the day's receipts when her phone buzzed.

Let's go away for the weekend. How about next weekend we go to Telluride, Colorado? I want to spoil you.

Could this day possibly get any better? First, her new tires. Next, her praise from Alexis, setting her on a path toward her dream. Now Boone wanted to spoil her. She felt like the luckiest woman alive today.

Take me away, cowboy. I'm yours.

She couldn't wait to go away with him, some place where they could be alone all weekend, trapped inside like they'd been on Sunday. No one would have ever guessed she'd fall so deeply for someone who was different from her, but on the other hand exactly like her.

She said goodbye to Alexis, who promised to update her, and headed to her car. Shoppers were out in force today, so she'd had to park a block away from the boutique. As she walked, up ahead in the distance she spotted the back of Boone's head as he entered Beaumont and Rossi's, the premier jewelry shop in Bronco Heights. It was the same place where Sofia had helped Jordan choose the honker of an engagement ring he'd given Camilla last year.

Suddenly, Sofia couldn't breathe. And then she started breathing too much. Of course, he might be getting her a tennis bracelet or something fun like that. Surely that was it. She was getting way ahead of herself. He'd already asked to take her away for the weekend. To spoil her. So it could be just a little sentimental gift. Nothing huge and life-changing like an engagement ring.

She texted Boone, knowing he'd be honest:

What are you doing right now?

His answer came a few seconds later:

Can't tell you, it's a big surprise.

She took in a few deep breaths, telling herself it didn't have to mean a marriage proposal.

Are you still coming by later for dinner?

She replied that she'd rather go out, suggesting DJ's Deluxe, which was practically their hangout. Sofia didn't think Boone would ask her to marry him in such a public place. That's probably why he'd made the reservations to go away together.

Surely he wouldn't… No. He wouldn't ask her to marry him, right? They'd already been over this, and he'd listened when she wanted to slow down, take her time. But a thought gnawed at her brain that every-thing was different now. They'd fallen in love. Love did extraordinary things to people, as she'd already seen with Jordan and Camilla.

Sofia was finally on her way to her dream, and marriage and children didn't fit in. Not now, and maybe not for a long time. She couldn't possibly get married now, but she also couldn't say no to Boone. That would really hurt him. She couldn't say no and still keep him. And she wanted to keep him. So she had to figure out a way she could.

For now, that meant she'd have to make excuses for why she couldn't go away next weekend.

Boone tucked his phone away and went back to the diamond rings that the owner had set out. This was the place where both Morgan and Holt had picked out their rings, so he knew they would have what he was looking for. A bright and shiny bling for the woman who'd stolen his heart. He'd already made the reservations next weekend at a five-star resort. The plan was to pop the question there on bended knee.

"May I ask who the lucky lady is?" The salesclerk was an older woman with graying hair and kind eyes.

He appreciated the vibe she gave off, like someone that could be trusted. Since he was about to make the most important decisions of his life, he wanted someone calm who could assure his racing heart that he was going to find and buy the perfect ring for the perfect woman.

"If you can be discreet."

The clerk went hand to chest as if she'd been injured. "I'm almost offended. This kind of information is top-secret around here."

"Okay, well, it's Sofia Sanchez. Do you know her? Do you know what she'd like?"

Maybe Boone should ask Camilla. He wanted to get the perfect ring, but he also wanted to get something unique. Special, just as she was. One of a kind.

"Of *course* I know Sofia." The clerk held up her finger and dived into another box. She opened it with a flourish. "These are some of the flashiest rings we have."

But they were all large and gaudy. Apparently,

the clerk didn't see Sofia the way he did. He couldn't see her wearing anything quite that…artless, in his opinion. The clerk kept bringing out boxes, noting carefully that each one was more expensive than the other, until he told her he lived at Dalton's Grange. After that, she didn't hold back. It took him several more minutes, but he found *the* ring. A two-carat solitaire diamond, surrounded by smaller encased stones: emerald, ruby and sapphire. Perfect for Sofia. Plenty of vibrant color for the woman who meant everything to him.

"This is the one." Boone paid and palmed the ring box into his leather jacket pocket.

He didn't know how he was going to resist giving it to her immediately, but he wanted the moment to be perfect. So he'd have to be patient. Next weekend couldn't come soon enough. Next week would arrive wrapped in possibilities. He'd make sure that she always remembered the moment he asked her to be his forever.

Boone drove home, amazed once more that his brothers' stupid prank had resulted in him finding true love like this. Not just a good time. Not just a beautiful woman to hang out with. He'd certainly had the last laugh. Thank God he'd gone into the store and met her, instead of brushing it all off as a mistake.

He stopped in at the family house to see his mother. She'd not so subtly indicated to him after

Sunday's dinner that she was impressed with Sofia. That he'd better straighten up his act, fly right and keep that treasure. And he intended to do just that.

He found her sitting before a crackling fire, a book on her lap. "Dinner should be ready in another hour."

"Thanks, but I didn't come by for that. I'm having dinner with Sofia."

She shut the book. "What's going on? I can see it's something huge."

His mother had always been able to read him. "How do you feel about having another daughter-in-law?"

"Boone!" She stood. "Are you serious?"

"I've never felt like this before. Yeah, I'm sure. She's it for me." His mother's eyes glistened with tears and he reached for her hand. "Wow, Mom, please don't cry."

"I'm sorry, honey. They're happy tears." She swiped at them as they ran down her cheeks. "I honestly never thought…you…"

"What?"

"I thought we'd ruined you for marriage, all of you boys. But I was especially worried about you. You've always been the peacekeeper in our family, and you had a lot of peace to make in those earlier years. Maybe I should have left your father then, I don't know, but I loved him. That's not so easy to walk away from. I had faith in him and hung in there."

"I don't know of anyone else who would have."

"You're right. It's rare to find unconditional love like what I feel for him." She went hand to heart. "He's my heart."

That's all Boone had ever wanted. To be the heart of a woman the way Neal was for his mother.

"You're a hell of a woman and a good example to me of love."

"Whatever you do, hang on to her. Never give up."

"She has to say yes, but I'll always put her first. Always. I know that Sofia wouldn't tolerate anything less than that."

Neal walked in then, his brow furrowed. He immediately came to his wife's side, rubbing her back. "What's this? Why are you crying?"

"Boone is going to propose," she replied.

"To Sofia? Well, well, that's something." He turned to Boone. "That's pretty fast."

"I just know," Boone said. "I'm ready for the first time in my life."

"And she's on the same page?" Neal asked.

"Who would say no to one of our boys?" his mother said.

"No one, I hope. If they know what's good for them. But there's no better man than Boone."

For the first time in a while, Boone felt that Neal's support was given without expecting anything in return. Not buying his forgiveness.

"Thanks, Dad." He met Neal's eyes, and something nameless clicked into place.

Boone wouldn't call it forgiveness, but a quiet type of understanding passed between them. They were both now men who'd experienced finding their soul mate, their true love, the one woman who'd changed them forever. A good thing to have in common with his father.

And Boone found this to be as good a place as any to start forgiving.

Chapter Seventeen

Boone arrived early to DJ's Deluxe and waited outside the entryway for Sofia. He'd rarely been this excited about life. The closest to this feeling might have been the time years ago when he'd retrained a horse that wound up winning in the National Rodeo. Loving Sofia had infused him with a jolt of energy.

All his plans for their life together played like a movie in his mind. In the past, he'd had an idealized version of the perfect wife. He'd realized lately that he'd always imagined himself marrying a woman not all that different from his mom—a woman who put home and family first. But he'd fallen hard for Sofia and had to admit that one of the main reasons was her passion for her work. He'd never ask her to give up her dream for him.

When she arrived, he hauled her into his arms, stepped to the side for privacy, and kissed her until he could feel the pattern of her breathing change.

"Oh, Boone. I missed you."

"Missed you, too." He trailed kisses down the column of her neck.

Taking her hand, he led her inside to see that DJ was already there to greet them. He clapped Boone on the back. "Haven't seen you two for a while. How are my favorite customers?"

"Favorite? How about regular?" Sofia laughed.

"I'm going to tell your sister you like my restaurant better than hers." DJ laughed as he walked them to their usual table.

"Don't you dare," Sofia said. "You're just closer to the boutique, that's all."

"Sure, sure," DJ said. "Admit it. No one can resist my potato skins."

"I had some not long ago at the Library, and let's just say you have some stiff competition, mister. Don't get cocky."

Sofia sat at their small table for two and as usual, Boone pulled up the chair close.

Not surprisingly, they were interrupted a few times by Sofia's friends, since she seemed to know everybody. Boone had already met more people through her than he had in the two years he'd been in Bronco. Brittany Brandt Dubois with her husband, Daniel, and their little girl, Hailey, stopped by on their way out. They were followed by Cassidy Ware and Brandon Taylor, whom Boone finally met for the first time. He had nothing to worry about in the way of an old boyfriend coming back around, because Brandon couldn't take his eyes off Cassidy.

Not that Boone had been at all concerned, but it was still good to see.

Their waitress came and took their orders and then they were finally alone.

"You know I love you, right?" Sofia said, giving him a small smile. "No matter what happens?"

"I would hope so. Why?" He narrowed his eyes, wondering where this would lead.

She reached for his hand and squeezed it. "Because I can't go away with you next weekend. I'm sorry but I forgot that I have a previous commitment. With Camilla."

"No problem. I'll just reschedule. How about the following weekend?"

"Um, yes, sure. I guess." She bit her fingernail, something he'd never seen her do, and a jolt of nameless alarm swept through him. Something was wrong. "I'll check with Alexis and see if that weekend is clear. She relies on me, you know. It's getting close to the holidays."

"Is that a problem?"

She pulled at her hair with her free hand. "There are a lot of personal stylings that go on for the huge holiday parties. The Association's holiday gala, that sort of thing."

That *damn* Association. Just the name irked him, and the way they'd denied his family membership.

"Doesn't Alexis have other help?"

"Yes, sure. She just prefers me."

Boone was fast losing his appetite. He could literally feel his shoulder muscles clench. "So do I. And it almost sounds like you're avoiding going away together."

Clearly, she didn't *want* to go away with him. She was making one lame excuse after the other. He couldn't understand what had happened, when and why she'd decided to pull back.

She let go of his hand. "Oh, guess what happened? I finally showed Alexis my portfolio, and she said she'd put me in touch with one of the designers she knows."

She'd circumvented his last statement with true skill. "Baby, that's so great. I'm happy for you."

She brightened. "It was easier than I thought it would be to ask for her opinion. I was worried she'd hate my designs."

"I'm surprised. You're always so confident."

"Well, sure, but this is so important to me. It's been a dream my whole life."

While he understood and encouraged her dream, he couldn't lie. He didn't love that her career seemed far more important to her than he did. He'd been supportive, and that would never stop, but he wanted to be a priority to her.

Just as she was for him.

"Tell me more about that dream." He rolled his shoulders, trying to ease the tightness there.

"I've already told you."

"Not in much detail. You mentioned a trip to New York City someday. I obviously know that you like your job. I've seen your designs and I know you're talented."

"I've worked so hard for this. I put myself through school at Montana State in the fashion design program. Got straight As. I've worked for Alexis since right after I got out of college. I'm always the first one at work and the last one to leave. I style all her best customers. I volunteer for the jobs no one else wants to do, like reading a hundred entries for the makeover contest. Alexis finds me indispensable. I figured that after I worked at the boutique for a few years, I could make contacts and find a way to get my designs into the hands of someone who could take me to that next level."

Boone swallowed. "The next level?"

"My own design label. It would be like having my own business. Vera Wang, Valentino, they all started that way. That's why it was so important to show Alexis my designs. To let her know I'm serious about this." Sofia spoke to him from under hooded lids.

He ran a hand down his face. His future plans were falling apart before they even got off the ground. His stomach rock hard, there would be no meal for him tonight. Even though he loved his work as a wrangler, and working with traumatized horses, he'd be willing to put Sofia first in everything. That happened when you really loved someone. But the feeling clearly wasn't mutual. And he was an idiot.

"Interesting how *I'm* not in any of your future plans. Us."

"That's not fair. Of course you are. I mean, you will be." She cleared her throat and bit her lower lip. "I'm just not ready for any of this. I love you, but I'm not…ready. For everything you seem to want. Marriage, children. I'm… Look, I think we should take a little break. I'm going to be busy these next few months, through the holidays. Not to mention that if I get any real interest in my designs, I'm going to have to put in a lot more hours of work on that end."

"You want to take a break. Now."

Sofia tapped her fingernails on the table and wouldn't look at him. "Just a little one."

Boone's heart beat hard enough to feel it in his eyes. This was all slipping away from him. She was slipping away. He couldn't help but think that if Sofia knew how serious he was about the two of them, she wouldn't want a break. Maybe she wasn't ready for a romance when she didn't know where this would lead in the end, but she'd appreciate the comfort and security of having a husband. Someone in her corner.

Yeah, he could do this.

This wasn't the way he'd wanted his proposal to go, and he'd left the ring at home, but a little spontaneity never killed anyone. He wasn't going to lose her without a fight.

He took both of her hands in his, feeling his own sweaty and clammy. "I don't want to take a break. I love you, and I want us to get married. Please, marry me."

Jerking back, she pulled her hands away. "Boone, no! I'm not ready for that. I love you, but I don't want to be someone's *wife*! I can't handle that right now. And I thought you understood."

But how was he supposed to understand when she'd failed to tell him that her career meant more to her than he did?

He didn't hear anything after her rejection. All the sounds in the restaurant, people chatting, glass clinking and silverware clattering, they all faded to black. Maybe if she saw the ring… No. Hell, no. If she didn't love him enough to marry him without seeing the rock he'd bought her, then he didn't want her to say yes.

"You're turning me down." Heat flushed through his body mixed with a heavy dose of shock.

He'd made plans. Told his parents. This was a disaster.

Sofia's voice was choked with tears and she tried to reach for his hand. "I didn't *want* to turn you down, which is why I told you I couldn't go away next weekend. Would you rather me say yes when I don't mean it? I have to be honest with you. I'm always honest."

"Honest? You lied about having plans with Camilla, didn't you? As long as we're being honest, this isn't what I want, either. You're halfway in this relationship. You keep taking a step back because you want it both ways. But I need someone who's willing to come along on a ride with me. For the rest of our lives. If that isn't you, and I can see now that it isn't, then I think we're through here."

With that he got up, left a hundred-dollar bill for whatever she'd want to order, and left.

He didn't once look back.

"Sofia, are you okay?"

Sofia looked up from the table and met the concerned eyes of DJ's wife, Allaire.

"I'm fine, why do you ask?" Sofia bit on her quivering lower lip as a single tear slid down her cheek.

"Because…you're crying?" Allaire kindly reached for Sofia's hands and squeezed them. "Did you and Boone have a fight?"

A doozy of a fight. A humdinger. Why had he asked her *here* of all places? Then again, it was the setting of their first date! Sofia nearly slapped her forehead. But Boone hadn't looked prepared, hadn't even shown her the ring, and the whole proposal seemed sudden. She couldn't understand why he'd decided to ask her then and there. Right after she'd told him she wanted a tiny break. It didn't make sense.

Sofia covered her eyes. "Yes, we had a fight. We broke up."

She couldn't stop seeing the surprised look on his face, his kind blue eyes narrowed and hurt. No one else probably had or ever would turn down Boone Dalton's proposal.

Allaire wrapped a comforting arm around Sofia's shoulders. "I'm sorry, honey. You two always looked so perfect together. The way he looks at you, he's completely smitten. If you wonder about his commitment to you, I'm sure all you need to do is have a talk. Anyone can see how much he loves you."

Sofia slid down her chair. Allaire didn't know how much worse she was making this for Sofia. Boone was everything she'd ever wanted, but he'd come along at the wrong time. And now she'd blown it because she wouldn't ever be able to have it all. Marriage, career, children. She'd had to make a choice, and she hadn't chosen him. The man she loved.

Unable to spill her guts here with everyone listening, Sofia couldn't be completely honest. "Sure, you're right. We'll work it out. It's just a little blip."

"That's the spirit." Allaire patted Sofia's back.

"In fact, I'm going to go catch him right now." Sofia stood up, needing Camilla more than she needed to breathe.

She almost couldn't drive, the emotions overtaking her, threatening to take her under a tidal wave of sadness. This wasn't what she'd wanted, after all. She'd wanted to keep him. Her lack of interest in marriage didn't mean she loved him any less. Why couldn't he see that? And yet someone like Boone, who'd had a hard time finding acceptance in this town, might feel especially rejected.

Like she didn't believe him good enough to marry. Nothing could be further from the truth, but how could she convince him of that when he'd walked away in a huff? He'd broken up with her and hadn't even heard what she'd said! She loved him and hadn't wanted to break things off. She'd just wanted more time.

Camilla didn't reply to Sofia's text, which likely meant another busy night at the Library. And what would Camilla have to say to her, anyway? That no one better than Boone would ever come along. That there would never be anyone she loved with as much intensity and heart. Everything Sofia already knew.

Feeling silly and immature, a young woman with her first real heartbreak, Sofia drove to her parents' home. She wanted her mother now, who would make her flan, the warm custard dessert with caramel syrup. She'd pat her hair like she had as a teenager. Sofia could always count on her mother. Even though Denise Sanchez worked six days a week at the salon, she had a rule to always be home for dinner. All the years Sofia had been growing up, the whole family gathered for dinner every single night of the week, even if the rest of the day was hit-or-miss.

Sofia would never dream of telling her mother, but there had been times when she'd wanted a parent on the school field trip. Or a mother who would volunteer as class mom. But her parents had both always worked, and though now she was proud of their work ethic, as a child she hadn't understood. Hadn't understood why her mother couldn't just quit her job and walk with her to her classroom instead of dropping her off at the school curb every morning with a kiss.

"What's wrong, *mija*?" her mother said the moment she opened the front door.

Sofia folded into her mother's arms and let the tears fall. Somehow, through the magic of motherhood, Sofia wound up on the couch a few seconds later, a warm fuzzy blanket thrown over her legs.

"What's going on here?" Her father's voice boomed when he entered the living room, hands on hips.

"Nothing, Aaron. I can handle this. Go find something to fix in the garage." Denise shooed him away.

"I won't be far," he grumbled as he walked away.

Her dear old dad. Always wanting to fix things for Sofia. Wanting only the best for her, as any girl's father should. The story went in their family lore that when baby Sofia was brought home from the hospital everyone wanted a turn holding her.

But Aaron wouldn't let anyone else hold her for at least a week, explaining that she was his littlest princess. By the end of the week, they'd all lost interest. Her mother swore that in those first few weeks

Sofia had been attached to her father every moment, except for feedings.

But though she'd always thought of herself as Daddy's girl, Sofia needed her mother tonight. She wanted the flan, the sympathy, and she didn't want anyone to try to fix this for her. Because she'd been the one to ruin everything, and it was her job to fix this. If anyone could.

Setting down the plate of flan and a glass of milk on the coffee table, her mother sat next to Sofia and smoothed down her hair. "This is a heartbreak, isn't it?"

"How do you know?"

"Mother's instinct."

The instinct had for once become useful as Sofia only had to nod her head. Words weren't necessary.

"I'm sorry, *mi amor.* You fell in love for the first time and it didn't work out. It will next time, you'll see. Did Boone break up with you?"

"Yes," Sofia said, taking a sip of milk.

"Well, if he doesn't see what a treasure you are, then he's not worth crying over, is he?"

"No, he *isn't!*" her father said, walking into the room again.

"Aaron!" her mother yelled. "I said go away. This is girl talk."

"Fine." He turned around in a huff.

"Oh, your father. You're his little princess and he wants to do something."

Sofia took a bite of flan, the warm custard settling in her tummy. "It was my fault. Boone asked me to marry him and I said no. When I said no, I hurt his feelings, and he just…broke up with me."

"What?" Her mother's eyes narrowed, confusion dotting their chocolate brown irises.

"I know you want me to get married, just like Camilla, but I'm not ready. I told him that. That I can't marry him now. I want a career. I don't want a husband and babies and all that. I'm sorry, *Mami*, I know you wanted that. But we're different."

"Don't apologize."

"I love him, and he knows that. But… I guess I humiliated him." She covered her face. "I didn't know how to say no to marriage and still keep him."

"And what on earth makes you think you can't have it all? *Mija*, you're a modern woman. You can have career *and* family."

"Real life makes me realize I can't have it all. Having it all is a myth. Whenever there are too many things vying for attention, some of them are going to get less than a hundred percent. I've already seen it happen with my job and my designs. I can't give my designs all of my time because I have a day job. That's probably why it's taken me so long to get where I am. What's going to happen when I have a job, a husband and maybe a child on the way? Huh?"

"Well, yes, it's a juggling act, of course. But some

balls are plastic and others are made out of glass. You can't drop the glass, but the plastic won't break."

The analogy made sense to Sofia, but it seemed all of her balls were made out of glass.

"I wanted all those things with him for the first time in my life. I wanted to be married and wake up every day next to the man I love. I wanted his babies. That's terrifying!"

"Why?"

"Because if he's already changed me this much, who am I going to be in a few years? Am I even going to recognize myself?"

"You're too worried about all of these things before they even happen. Besides, love does change you. That's normal and it's a good thing, as long as it changes you for the better. These are growing pains. You can't stay in one place too long or you'll grow cobwebs."

"It's just that I know what he wants, and I can't give it to him right now."

"I know you love him, but is he a good man? Someone you can count on? Strong?"

"Yes, he's all of those things. He's…perfect." Another tear slid down her cheek and she wiped it away.

"No one is perfect, and Boone just proved my point. I'm guessing he let his pride get away from him, or he would have taken the time to listen to you. If he loves you, he'll wait until you're ready for all of these things. Marriage, children." She threw Sofia a significant look. "Just like I'm waiting."

Sofia snorted. "Are you, though?"

"You may not think so, but I am. And I know that Camilla and Jordan aren't having babies any-time soon. She didn't have to tell me that. Things are different from when I was young woman in Mexico. Women have choices now, and that's a good thing. I think it makes for a more confusing life, all those choices, but that's not for me to say. I'm old school, as you kids say."

Sofia wondered if these really were growing pains, and if so, why was she so afraid of changing? Change wasn't always a negative thing. Even if her mind tried to dismiss the fact that she'd fallen in love at first sight, her heart knew the truth. It made sense to resist all the upheaval when it all happened so quickly.

But she wouldn't be much of a modern woman if she didn't make room in her life for love.

No matter when it showed up.

Chapter Eighteen

The next morning, Boone woke up on the floor of his cabin when something cold and wet tickled his nose. He jerked, finding Spot sitting beside him expectantly, head cocked as he eyed him. Boone had a headache the size of Texas and a ball of cotton stuck to the roof of his mouth. Or maybe it just seemed that way.

"What am I doing on the floor?" He groaned, straightening.

"Yark!" Spot said in answer, which was not helpful.

Then Boone remembered. He'd been about to make coffee around three in the morning but decided he was too sleepy. Even too tired to walk to the couch, apparently. He'd slid down the wall of the cupboard and had only meant to close his eyes for a minute or two.

He found Thing 1 and Thing 2, one sprawled on the couch, the other on the floor surrounded by pillows. A half-empty bottle of tequila sat on the end table. Pieces of the evening rushed back to him. Too much tequila. An argument over who could bench-press more weight. Then about something having to do with Marvel Studios. Another about...*The Blues Brothers*? He scratched his jaw. Gratefully, he didn't remember speaking a word about Sofia. If his brothers had wondered where she was, they didn't ask.

But Boone would bet that his parents had already told Shep and Dale that Boone had had plans to go away with Sofia next weekend and ask her to marry him. He refused to talk about it with anyone. It was done. Over. He'd have to move on.

The whole experience left him shell-shocked and not ready to fall in love again anytime soon. He couldn't understand where he'd gotten it all so wrong. Why, if Sofia loved him as she said, she'd turned him down. He'd had the guts to risk it all, and she couldn't even meet him halfway. His heart ached more than he'd ever imagined possible, and his chest felt like it had been kicked by a Clydesdale.

Boone staggered to the kitchen and inhaled a water bottle, then crunched it in one hand. The cotton in his mouth eased up a little, but not by much. He started the coffee and when it was brewed, he poked Shep.

"Whaaa?" He rolled over and squinted. "Where am I?"

"The twenty-first century. Bronco, Montana. Why did you let me drink tequila?"

"Those are a lot of questions all at once." He cradled his head.

Boone rolled his eyes. "Right. Here, have some coffee, and get out of my house."

Next Dale rose from the floor, looking like he'd been through a tsunami. His hair was disheveled, and his chin sported about a month's worth of beard growth, which wasn't possible. Hairy guy.

"What happened last night?" he asked.

"Too much tequila is my guess," Boone replied. "Grab some coffee."

"Wait. I remember something," Shep said from the couch. "We found you mucking the stalls. Shoveling manure like it was your worst enemy. Cursing. You sure were in a bad mood. What's wrong? A fight with Sofia?"

"I don't want to talk about it."

"Oh, yeah. A fight. You guys had a fight. What about?" Shep said, giving Dale a sideways glance. "I hope it wasn't about that account we set up. No one should really know about that."

"Can't be. They just started interviewing," Dale said. "It's too early."

Boone instantly perked up. "What account? What interview?"

His brothers exchanged a look.

"Don't kill us." Dale threw his palms up. "But you made it too easy. All we had to do was photoshop a red rose in your hand."

"It was Dale's idea," Shep said. "He's vying to be the king of pranks."

"What did you guys do?" Boone ran a hand down his face in frustration.

Dale pulled his phone out, scrolled and handed it to Boone. "They're looking for a new Mr. Montana."

The regional TV show where a bachelor auditioned single women to be his future wife was far from anything Boone would ever consider. There in vivid color was a photo of him, one of the ones from the photo shoot at BH Couture. He wore the tight suit Sofia loved him in and a smile on his face which he vividly recalled had been because he'd been flirting with Sofia off camera. She'd put him at ease that day, as she had on all the others. Made him think that she really cared. Fooled him.

"Wealthy rancher ready to settle down with Mrs. Right" was written atop the photo.

"Take it down." He handed the phone back to Dale. "Now."

"You made it through the first round."

"What do you expect? You *advertised* that I'm wealthy."

Unlike Sofia, who'd liked him when she thought he was a poor ranch hand.

"Okay, it was all in good fun. Anyway, we signed you up before we knew how serious you were about Sofia. Next up was the interview, and we figured we'd take it down by then if you got that far. But hey, maybe Sofia won't work out, and you might want a backup plan. Have you *seen* the women that apply to these shows?" Dale made the shape of a curvy woman with his hands. "Hot!"

"Then why don't you apply?"

Dale held up both his palms. "Are you kidding? I don't want to get married!"

"Sofia and I broke up, but I don't want to be on that ridiculous show. You can do whatever you need to do, but take this down before someone else in town sees it."

"How did you blow it with her?" Dale asked.

"What makes you think *I* blew it?"

"Um, because you're a guy?" Shep shrugged.

"Okay, genius. Not this time! She said she loved me. And I love her, so I asked her to marry me. She said no."

"Are you out of your mind?" Shep's voice reverberated in the room. His brother looked horrified. "How long have you known her? Five minutes?"

"When you know it's right, you don't have to sit around and watch paint dry."

"You're an idiot," Dale said, shaking his head.

"Hey, I want a wife and a family. A woman who doesn't mind a man who wants to take care of her. I mean, look at Morgan and Holt. They've both got ready-made families. That's what I want, too. A wife. Kids. The whole deal."

"You're certifiably insane, brother. You've got a beautiful woman who wants you, but doesn't want to get married, and you threw that all away?" Dale shook his head as if in disbelief.

"If a wife and family is what you really want, you should leave the profile up," Shep said. "You'll be married in no time."

"But I don't want anyone else."

At those words, Boone took a long, hard look at the facts. Easy to do because they'd just slapped him across the face. He'd said the words out loud and suddenly he *heard* them.

If he simply wanted to get married and get his family started, he'd sign up with a dating site. Sort through all the women and find one who honestly liked him. Maybe he'd find one that he connected with on some level. Of course, it wouldn't be that easy. He couldn't even look at another woman because he only wanted Sofia. Which meant, of course, that he'd been an idiot to break up with her. All she wanted was time and he'd let his injured pride get in the way. He'd pushed forward, thinking only of what *he* wanted, and on *his* timeline.

Somehow, he'd forgotten that she also had a say in their future together, if they were to have one at all.

"Why not just go to her and tell her you made a mistake? That you don't want to break up after all?" Dale asked.

"She's never going to forgive me now. Are you kidding? I broke up with her and just walked out."

The memory of that moment brought him new

pain. He was a man who had learned patience the hard way, who relearned it every day when he worked with an overwhelmed and traumatized horse. Every injured animal recovered on their own timetable. Every colt and filly learned at their own pace. He couldn't rush things even if he wanted to.

He'd made the cardinal mistake of a newbie wrangler. Asking for too much, too soon.

A few days later, Boone had thrown himself into his work. He'd taken on new clients, filling up his roster so he'd be busy 24/7. Having stayed away from town, he hadn't run into anyone who knew Sofia or had seen the two of them together.

To add insult to injury, his buddy Spot seemed to be missing. Maybe he'd gone back to his original owner, though Boone hadn't been able to find one. He'd meant to ask Daphne at Happy Hearts if she could put some feelers out, but maybe he'd stalled because he'd gotten too attached to Spot.

Either way, he'd taken several long rides on the property with Burrito, searching for the little guy with no luck. Maybe he'd be back in a day or so. It just didn't seem fair for a guy to lose his girl and his dog in the same week. Great. He was officially a country-and-western song.

He shook the dust off his Stetson and reentered the corral where he'd been working with the new colt he'd been breaking for Neal, the one he'd named DG after Dalton's Grange. The horse had shown his true colors on day one. He'd reared back in fear, nearly knocking Boone off his feet.

"You're a pain in my ass, you know?" Boone had said softly, after making soothing sounds. "I should call you Sofia."

Today, he was running DG in the corral, letting him spend his energy. He had a saddle on for the first time, and though he'd allowed it, he didn't like it. DG kept trying to shake it off, bucking like a wild horse. Boone didn't want to ruin him by trying to mount him too soon, so he'd wait him out.

"You ready for this weekend?" From the other side of the fence corral, his father shouted to him.

Boone walked to the side of the corral to meet his father. "This weekend?"

"You're going to pop the question."

He'd almost forgotten. Call it denial but after canceling the reservations on time, he'd stopped torturing himself with the memory.

"No, Dad, the engagement isn't happening."

All the color seemed to drain from his father's face. "What happened?"

"She couldn't get away this weekend, so I asked her a few nights ago. Turned me down."

Neal removed his Stetson and raked a hand through his hair. "I was worried about that when you told your mother and me. Ironically, you're the son that's most like your old man. I also asked your mother too soon and got turned down flat."

"What? Mom turned you down? When? How? Why?"

"Don't laugh but when I say I asked too soon, well, I asked her to marry me the day we met."

"*Excuse* me?"

"I've always been a man who knew what he wanted and didn't want to waste any time." He met Boone's eyes. "Sound familiar?"

Unfortunately, it did. "I don't know why, but I have patience in the corral. Why can't I be patient about other stuff?"

"Love makes a man crazy. I know it did me. But I waited your mother out. How about that, your old man had patience. Well, she taught me how. When I asked her a few months later, she said yes. Give Sofia time, and if she loves you, she'll come around."

"I shouldn't have walked out on her."

"Did you?"

"Too proud, I guess. I thought if she turned me down for marriage, I should stop wasting my time."

"Your mother would say it's never a waste of time to love someone."

"It hurt, and I was humiliated."

"No one understands that better than your old man." He lowered his head. "I hope it wasn't me and my reputation that ruined this for you."

Neal sounded genuinely sorry, and something

shifted in Boone's chest. His father didn't deserve all the constant recriminations made against him. He'd made a few mistakes in his life, but who hadn't? If there was a perfect person somewhere, Boone had yet to meet him. And Neal had walked through fire to make it up to his wife. To his family. With all that money, he could have walked away and started over without them.

"No, it wasn't about you. And anyone else who has a problem with you is going to have to answer to me from now on."

He'd stood up for his brothers, and now he would for his father, a man who'd been punished enough. Especially by him.

"Thank you, son. It means more to me than I can say. But I don't happen to care what anyone else thinks. Just you."

Boone let the acknowledgment slide into him. He had the respect of his father and could now give it back. An idea had been ruminating in him for a few days, something he never thought he'd accept.

"Remember when you said you'd like to do something for me?"

Neal clapped a hand on Boone's shoulder. "Anything. You're talented and anyone can see your gift after watching you work for a few minutes. You want more land for the wild horses, well, I think there's a way we can make that work from a business perspective. Maybe form a coalition of horse ranchers. I have some other ideas, too."

"Actually, what I'd like is for you to think about investing in a fashion line."

Neal wrinkled his brow. "A *what*?"

"Fashion line. I happen to know a young and talented designer who's trying to find her way into the big leagues. She's got a business plan and an amazing work ethic. She's talented. She's going places."

"Uh-huh. Sofia, right?"

Boone nodded. "Business is more your wheelhouse than it's mine. This is what she wants. And I love her, so I want her to have her dream."

"Let me do some research, make some calls. I'm just a rancher but I do know a few businessmen I've met over the years. They might give me some direction. If this is what you want, son, you've got it."

"But I don't want you to do anything to risk your holdings. This should be because you see it as a good investment, not only as a favor to me. She wouldn't have it any other way."

"You really love her, don't you? Does she feel the same way?"

"She says she does, but I don't know. I guess I didn't give her time to explain. I didn't hear anything she said after 'no.'"

And with every day that passed, his idiocy became more apparent. He might be a horse whisperer, but he sure didn't understand people enough.

* * *

Sofia popped into DJ's Deluxe all week hoping she might run into Boone. But it seemed he'd made himself scarce. Once, she thought she'd seen him walking down Main Street, but it was another cowboy.

The weekend he'd invited her to go away came and went. Sofia would be an engaged woman if she'd gone along with it. And maybe she'd be happier than she was these days, doing nothing but working and sketching. She'd been asked out twice at work, both times by guys in wing tips. Not a single hot cowboy. It didn't matter. She couldn't think of dating anyone right now, or for a long time.

Meanwhile, initial feedback on her designs from Alexis's contacts were promising, but it would be a while before she heard anything more.

Her life felt dull and flat, like muted colors, a boring beige.

She'd decided that if Boone changed his mind, if he wanted to talk, she'd forgive his Neanderthal ways in a second. If he really loved her, he'd come to the realization that he should at least try to understand her point of view. She wanted to marry him. Someday. She certainly loved him, if that counted for anything. And she couldn't help but believe that it should.

Meanwhile, the holiday stylings had started, and BH Couture was as usual in high demand with

Bronco's elite. Sofia dressed Jessica Taylor in a ravishing blue sequined Vera Wang with matching shoes. Cassidy had come in, too, reluctantly and somewhat insecure. But she'd be attending these big galas with Brandon, so she wanted to look her best and be fashionable. She'd come to the right place.

During a temporary lull, Alexis marched to Sofia holding up her phone. "Hey, isn't this Boone? This is from our photo shoot! How dare they? These photos are the property of BH Couture. I should sue!"

"Why? What's wrong?" Sofia took the phone Alexis held out, and there in living color was Boone, holding a red rose.

Someone was certainly talented with photoshop. He'd apparently applied for the *Mr. Montana* TV show. Wealthy Rancher Seeks Mrs. Right. She remembered the photo. He'd smiled directly at her off camera as he modeled his new clothes. Later that night, he'd kissed her until she could barely remember her name.

The ache Sofia had been nursing for the past week rose to the surface. Clearly, Boone wanted a wife and nothing more. He didn't want her. He didn't want a partner, didn't want a lover, didn't want a friend. He wanted a *wife*. Pure and simple. And love didn't seem to matter much to him. *Waiting* must be a word not in his vocabulary.

"What's he doing applying to the show? I thought you two were an item." Alexis took back her phone.

"We were," Sofia said around the sob in her throat.

"I'm sorry."

"Don't be. It's clear that he knows exactly what he wants."

"Maybe he won't get chosen for the show. They have lots of rounds to get through."

Sofia nodded, but that was hardly the point.

Chapter Nineteen

At the end of a long day, Sofia went home to her apartment, hoping to put this rotten day behind her. She wouldn't hear from Boone again, and she couldn't blame him. He knew what he wanted, so he'd moved on. But just the thought of him being picked for that show, with all those gorgeous women vying for his attention, made her stomach churn. If that's what he wanted, a made-to-order bride, he could have her. Maybe it was too difficult for him to have a relationship with someone who had her own mind. While that didn't sound like the Boone she knew and loved, she had to accept the truth.

The truth was that he'd dropped her when she didn't want to get married. If he truly loved her, he'd wait for her. Just like *Mami*, who understood unconditional love. Boone could learn a thing or two from his own mother. She'd forgiven a lot more. He could have accepted Sofia just as she was, a woman who felt on the brink of her dream career. Marriage and children would have come eventually with Boone. Now she didn't know if she'd ever want to find love again. Unlike Boone, who was already lining up auditions for her replacement.

She should be angry, but instead her heart ached.

Only Boone had made her feel confident when pared down to the bare essentials. She was confident in her own skin, but she'd never felt *truly* beautiful, until Boone.

Forgive. I'm not good at that.

She remembered him saying that as they danced that afternoon at his house. She should have heard him and taken him at his word. If he hadn't forgiven his own father after years, he'd probably never be able to forgive her.

Frustrated and aching, she entered her apartment, gathering her mail and tossing it on the table as she took off her coat and hung it up. She thought she was facing another long night, alone with a TV dinner and her sketches, till she caught sight of the package that had come in the mail. The face mask she'd been waiting for. Quickly she opened it, realizing it was just what she needed. When in doubt, exfoliate! She wasted no time. She pulled back her hair into a high ponytail, washed her face and applied the green mask. Setting the timer, she went to the freezer to see if she had any comfort food. Her phone buzzed when she was in the middle of scooping salted caramel ice cream into a bowl. At the same time, there was a knock at her door.

"Great timing, whoever you are," Sofia muttered

as she walked to the door and glanced at her phone. She gasped at the message from the man who was listed in her contacts as My Cowboy.

Answer the door. You might not miss my texts, but I miss yours. I'm an idiot.

It was official! Boone Dalton had the worst timing in the history of history.

She texted back. You are 100% right about being an idiot, but I can't see you right now. Come back later, Mr. Montana. Leave a rose at the door and walk away.

"I can't do that," he groaned from the other side of her door. "This can't wait."

This time she didn't bother with a text. "Cowboy," she called through the door, "you have really lousy timing, you know that?"

"Yes, when it comes to you. But I'm not going anywhere. You do have to come out eventually. I'll stay outside until you're ready."

How about that—until she was *ready*. Would wonders never cease.

"Uh-huh. What if I'm not ready until tomorrow? You're going to sleep out there all night in the cold?"

"Throw me a blanket and I'm good."

But he sounded so disgusted with himself, so dejected, that a jolt of sympathy hit her hard and swift. She wanted to see him.

Sofia threw open the door and crossed her arms. "What can I do for you?"

His head jerked back, but then he looked dangerously close to smiling. His mouth twitched at the corners.

"Don't!" She held up her finger. "Don't laugh. As you can see, I wasn't expecting anyone."

"First, I'm not auditioning for the *Mr. Montana* show. Let me get that out of the way. That was another one of my brothers' pranks. I had them take it down when I found out about it."

When she moved aside, he ambled in, shutting the door behind him.

"Good, because I don't know if you have the scoop on those shows, but I do. And I don't see how anyone can find a wife or husband with *that* kind of pressure."

He winced. "Point taken."

Boone looked so wonderful in his leather jacket, boots, jeans and Stetson. So familiar. A day's worth of beard growth dotted his square jaw. Just the sight of him made her ache to hold him and pick up right where they'd left off. But she forced herself to hold her ground.

"What do you want?" she said, remembering how he'd walked out on her at DJ's Deluxe.

"To apologize in person." He took off his hat and yanked a hand through that amazing tousled hair. "I let my pride get in the way when you said no to my proposal. To be honest, it was spontaneous. You might have guessed I'd planned to ask you on the weekend we were going away. But that night at DJ's Deluxe, I thought I was about to lose you, and I couldn't stand the thought."

"You weren't—"

He held up a hand, palm out. "Let me finish. When you said no to me, well, I didn't hear anything after that. You said you loved me, but I didn't believe you could really mean that."

"Boone, I don't toss that word around. I've only ever said it to family members. You're the first man I ever fell in love with and I'd hoped you would be the last."

"That's all I want. I didn't care whether I was your first, but I want to be your last."

Her heart softened and she lowered her arms to her side. "Don't you want a *wife* right this second?"

"I want *you*, Sofia, however I can have you. I'm not going to lie. I do want all those things, marriage and babies. But I don't want any of that if I can't have it with you."

Those sweet and perfect words sliced right through her in a tender ache.

"When you say things like that it's hard to stay mad at you." She took a step toward him. This cowboy was her whole heart. She'd never be happy without him at her side. "Boone, I never wanted to take a break from us. I think I just freaked out a little bit."

"Look, I'll be patient and hope that someday you catch up to me. In the long run, I know we want the same things." He smiled. "And I love you, green face and all."

Sofia blinked. She'd been so caught up in his words of love that she'd actually forgotten about the clay mask. She didn't know if she should laugh or cry.

She touched her face. "Oh, my Lord."

"C'mere, Mrs. Shrek, and let me kiss you." He tossed his hat to the couch.

Crazy with love and lust, Sofia jumped into his arms, and he caught her easily.

Cradling his face, she kissed him hard and when she pulled back, his nose, cheeks and beard were slightly green. She ran a hand across his jaw, wiping some of the color away. She'd never let a man see her exfoliate before today, or shared her beauty secrets with him. But Boone had created a lot of firsts for her. And she looked forward with all her heart to many more firsts.

"Forgive me?" He squeezed her tighter.

That part was easy. He'd come back to her, even when she couldn't give him everything he wanted right now. He was offering her just what she needed.

Unconditional love.

"Yes, I forgive you. You're the only man I ever let see the real me. I love you, Boone Dalton, and I want to get married and have your babies. Someday."

She pressed her forehead to his. "You're the only one for me. Forever."

"Whenever you're ready, you let me know. I have the ring. No pressure."

She'd been curious about that ring since she'd seen him walk into the jewelry store.

But now it was her turn to be patient.

Boone couldn't believe his fortune. Earlier today, Spot had shown up at the ranch again. Now, Sofia had forgiven him. His brothers were right for once. He ought to note the date and the time.

He set Sofia back on her feet. "But wait. There's more."

She smiled, tugging on his belt. "There is more, but first I'd like to wash this mask off. Then I'm going to attack you."

The realization that she'd missed him as much as he'd missed her spiked him with desire. She took his hand and led him to the kitchen sink, where she wet a paper towel and then turned to wipe his face.

Boone couldn't wait. He started to tell her his news before she'd finished. "Remember I said that my father wanted to do something to help me? He's been hounding me ever since I moved to Bronco."

"He wanted to help you to start your own horse rescue business." She took another paper towel and wiped her own face, the green muck coming off in thick streaks.

And to think she hadn't liked him seeing her without makeup their first night together. She'd never looked more gorgeous to him than at this moment. Knowing that she trusted him enough to let him see her at what she would consider her worst was everything he needed to know. She was his and he was hers. No going back now, or ever.

He took the paper towel from her and wiped her nose and cheeks until he only saw the milky color of her clear skin.

"But I think it's pretty clear I'm happy with the work I already have. I'm a horse whisperer and maybe, someday, a horse rescuer."

"Did you tell him that?"

"In a way. You should know that I forgave my father. It wasn't easy. It never is for me. But I know deep down he's a good family man who made a terrible mistake. And he's more than made up for it."

She framed his face. "I'm so happy for you."

"Anyway, I asked him to do something else for me instead. I talked to him about a talented designer I know." He tugged on a lock of her hair.

"Who, me?"

"Yes, you. I asked him to invest in you. As your first big financial backer. And the thing is, he said yes. He believes in you as much as I do. So you have a backer to start you own clothing line or boutique, whenever you're ready."

"Seriously? Oh, Boone. Thank you for believing in me."

"You believed in me first, when you tried to give me a total fashion makeover."

"Until I realized you're perfect just the way you are."

"Not perfect, never perfect." He took her hand and brushed a kiss across her knuckles. "But definitely yours."

"I'll take you."

He swept her off her feet, carrying her to bed. Their first time had been an explosion of heat and anger, turning into a fiery passion that fueled them all night long. Now they were both tentative and slow. Tender. For his part, he wanted to appreciate the moment, knowing he'd almost lost this treasure. This woman who loved him for himself and not what he owned.

He still had a lot of work ahead to forge a stronger relationship with his father. Sofia had already given him the start. She was undoubtedly his best friend.

Gently he laid her on the bed, her red hair fanning around her like a halo. He was so in love with this woman. Slowly, he removed her clothes, kissing each swath of soft flesh as he went. Lips, the shell of her ear, neck, shoulders. He spent time on each nipple, licking and sucking until she moaned and squirmed. The sounds she made lit a blaze in him, and his vow to take it slow went out the window. They reached for each other, tugging, straining, desperate to get closer.

Sofia pulled at his shirt with such force that one of the buttons ripped. "Oh, sorry."

"Don't ever be sorry about that."

He tried to slow them down, but with a naked Sofia bucking and writhing under him, he wondered if they would *ever* have a low-flame setting. Definitely not tonight. They could try again another time. Now he ripped open a condom and plunged into her. She gasped, moaning and meeting him thrust for thrust.

"You're taking me on a wild ride, aren't you?" he whispered, his breaths ragged.

"Always."

Boone could always feel when she got close to her release, and only then did he let go of his tight control. He went over the crest with her, moaning her name.

Arms wrapped around her tightly, he eventually managed to slow his breathing.

"That was incredible," Sofia gasped. "Crazy."

"Unbelievable."

"Will it always be this way between us?" Her voice sounded for once weak and even a little bit worried. "Can it?"

He pressed a kiss to her temple. "Yes. I'll make sure of it."

"Boone, I can't believe I'm so lucky. You entered a contest, but I won the prize."

Well, that was one thing they could argue about for the rest of their lives, because right now he certainly felt like the grand-prize cowboy.

* * * * *

*Look for the next book in the new
Harlequin Special Edition continuity
Montana Mavericks:
The Real Cowboys of Bronco Heights*

A Kiss at the Mistletoe Rodeo
by Kathy Douglass

*On sale November 2021 wherever
Harlequin books and ebooks are sold.*

*And catch up with the previous
Montana Mavericks titles:*

The Rancher's Summer Secret
by New York Times *bestselling author
Christine Rimmer*

For His Daughter's Sake
by USA TODAY *bestselling author
Stella Bagwell*

The Most Eligible Cowboy
by Melissa Senate

Available now!

HARLEQUIN

*Uplifting or passionate,
heartfelt or thrilling—
Harlequin has your
happily-ever-after.*

With a wide range of romance series that each
offer new books every month, you are sure to
find the satisfying escape you deserve.

**Look for all Harlequin series
new releases on the
last Tuesday of each month
in stores and online!**

Harlequin.com

COMING NEXT MONTH FROM

(H) HARLEQUIN

SPECIAL EDITION

#2869 THE FATHER OF HER SONS
Wild Rose Sisters • by Christine Rimmer
Easton Wright now wants to be part of his sons' lives—with the woman he fell hard for during a weeklong fling. Payton Dahl doesn't want her sons to grow up fatherless like she did, but can she risk trusting Easton when she's been burned in the past?

#2870 A KISS AT THE MISTLETOE RODEO
Montana Mavericks: The Real Cowboys of Bronco Heights
by Kathy Douglass
During a rare hometown visit to Bronco for a holiday competition, rodeo superstar Geoff Burris is sidelined by an injury—and meets Stephanie Brandt. Geoff is captivated by the no-nonsense introvert. He'd never planned to put down roots, but when Stephanie is in his arms, all he can think about is forever...

#2871 TWELVE DATES OF CHRISTMAS
Sutter Creek, Montana • by Laurel Greer
When a local wilderness lodge almost cancels its Twelve Days of Christmas festival, Emma Halloran leaps at the chance to convince the owners of her vision for the business. But Luke Emerson has his own plans. As they work together, Luke and Emma are increasingly drawn to each other. Can these utter opposites unite over their shared passion this Christmas?

#2872 HIS BABY NO MATTER WHAT
Dawson Family Ranch • by Melissa Senate
Nothing will change how much Colt Dawson loves his baby boy. Not even the shocking news his deceased wife lied about Ryder's paternity. But confronting Ava Guthrie about his ex's sperm-donor scheme doesn't go as planned. Will Ava heal Colt's betrayed heart in time for a Wyoming family Christmas?

#2873 THE BEST MAN IN TEXAS
Forever, Texas • by Marie Ferrarella
Jason Eastwood and Adelyn Montenegro may have hit it off at a wedding, but neither of them is looking for love, not when they have careers and lives to establish. Still, as they work together to build the hospital that's meaningful to them both, the pull between them becomes hard to resist. Will they be able to put their preconceived ideas about relationships aside, or will she let the best man slip away?

#2874 THE COWBOY'S CHRISTMAS RETREAT
Top Dog Dude Ranch • by Catherine Mann
Riley Stewart has been jilted. He needs an understanding shoulder, so Riley invites his best friend, Lucy Snyder, to join him on his "honeymoon." But moonlit walks, romantic fires, the glow of Christmas lights—everything is conspiring against their "just friends" resolve. Will this fake honeymoon ignite the real spark Riley and Lucy have denied for so long?

YOU CAN FIND MORE INFORMATION ON UPCOMING HARLEQUIN TITLES, FREE EXCERPTS AND MORE AT HARLEQUIN.COM.

HSECNM1021

SPECIAL EXCERPT FROM

H HARLEQUIN
SPECIAL EDITION

Nothing will change how much Colt Dawson loves his baby boy. Not even the shocking news his deceased wife lied about Ryder's paternity. But confronting Ava Guthrie about his ex's sperm-donor scheme doesn't go as planned. Will Ava heal Colt's betrayed heart in time for a Wyoming family Christmas?

Read on for a sneak peek at
His Baby No Matter What,
the next book in the Dawson Family Ranch miniseries by Melissa Senate!

"I wasn't planning on getting one," Ava said. "I figured it would be make me feel sad, celebrating all alone out at the ranch. My parents gone too young. And this year, my great-aunt gone before I even knew her. My best friend after the worst argument I've ever had. I love Christmas, but this is a weird one."

"Yeah, it is. And you're not alone. I'm here. Ryder's here. And like you said, you love Christmas. That house needs some serious cheering up. I want to get you a tree as a gift from me to you for our good deal."

"It *is* a good deal," she said. "Okay. A tree. I have a box of ornaments that I brought over in the move to the ranch."

He pulled out his phone, did some googling and found a Christmas-tree farm that also sold wreaths just ten minutes from here. He held up the site. "Let's go after Ryder's nap. While he's asleep, we can have that meeting—I mean, *talk*—about our arrangement. Set the agenda. The… What would you call it in noncorporate speak?"

She laughed. "Maybe it is a little nice having a CEO around here," she said, then took a bite of her sandwich. "You get things done, Colt Dawson."

He reached over and touched her hand and she squeezed it. Again he was struck by how close he felt to her. But he had to remember he was leaving in two and a half weeks, going back to Bear Ridge, back to his life. There was a 5 percent chance, probably less, that he'd ever leave Godfrey and Dawson. But he'd have this break, this Christmas with his son, on this alpaca ranch.

With a woman who made him think of reaching for the stars, even if he wouldn't.

Don't miss
His Baby No Matter What *by Melissa Senate,*
available November 2021 wherever
Harlequin Special Edition books and ebooks are sold.

Harlequin.com